SUPERHERO STAMPEDE

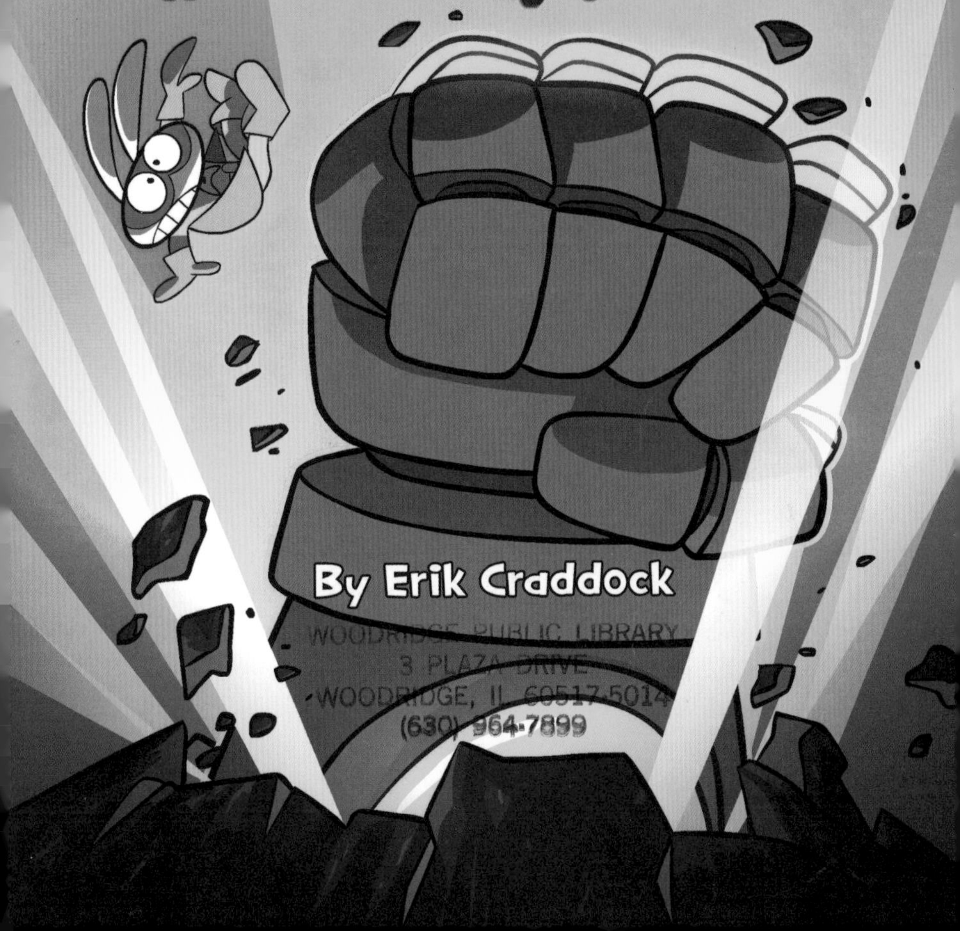

By Erik Craddock

Published in the United States by Random House Children's Books, a division of Random House, Inc., New York. Random House and the colophon are registered trademarks of Random House, Inc.
Visit us on the Web! www.randomhouse.com/kids
Educators and librarians, for a variety of teaching tools, visit us at www.randomhouse.com/teachers
www.stonerabbit.com
Library of Congress Cataloging-in-Publication Data
Craddock, Erik.
Superhero stampede / by Erik Craddock. — 1st ed.
p. cm. — (Stone Rabbit ; 4)
Summary: After being zapped by a home-made reality transmutation device, Stone Rabbit and his friends find themselves inside the pages of their favorite comic book, waging war against a band of evildoers and trying to save the world.
ISBN 978-0-375-85877-2 (pbk.) — ISBN 978-0-375-95877-9 (lib. bdg.)
1. Graphic novels. [1. Graphic novels—Fiction. 2. Rabbits—Fiction. 3. Cartoons and comics—Fiction. 4. Superheroes—Fiction. 5. Humorous stories.] I. Title.
PZ7.7.C73Su 2010
741.5'973—dc22
2009036834
MANUFACTURED IN MALAYSIA
10 9 8 7 6 5 4 3 2 1
First Edition

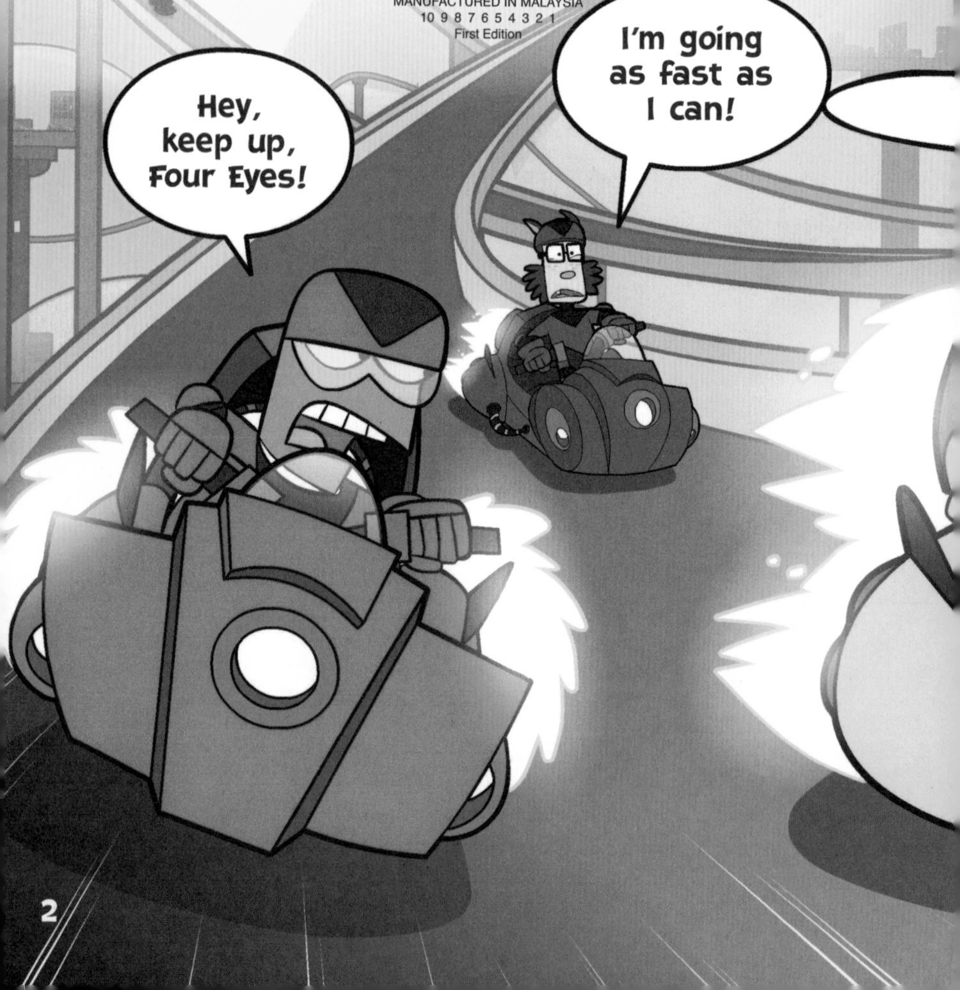
Hey, keep up, Four Eyes!
I'm going as fast as I can!

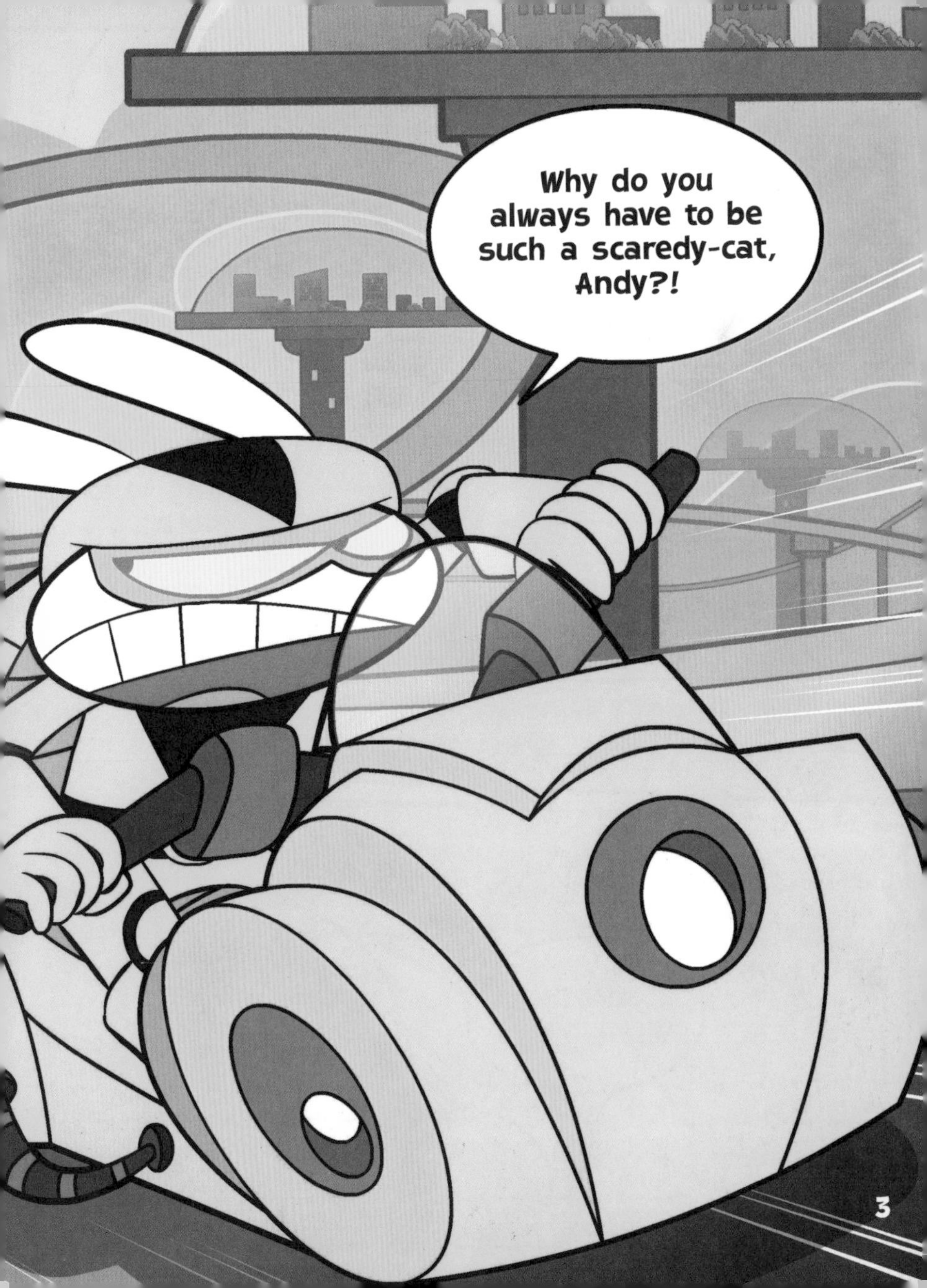
Why do you always have to be such a scaredy-cat, Andy?!

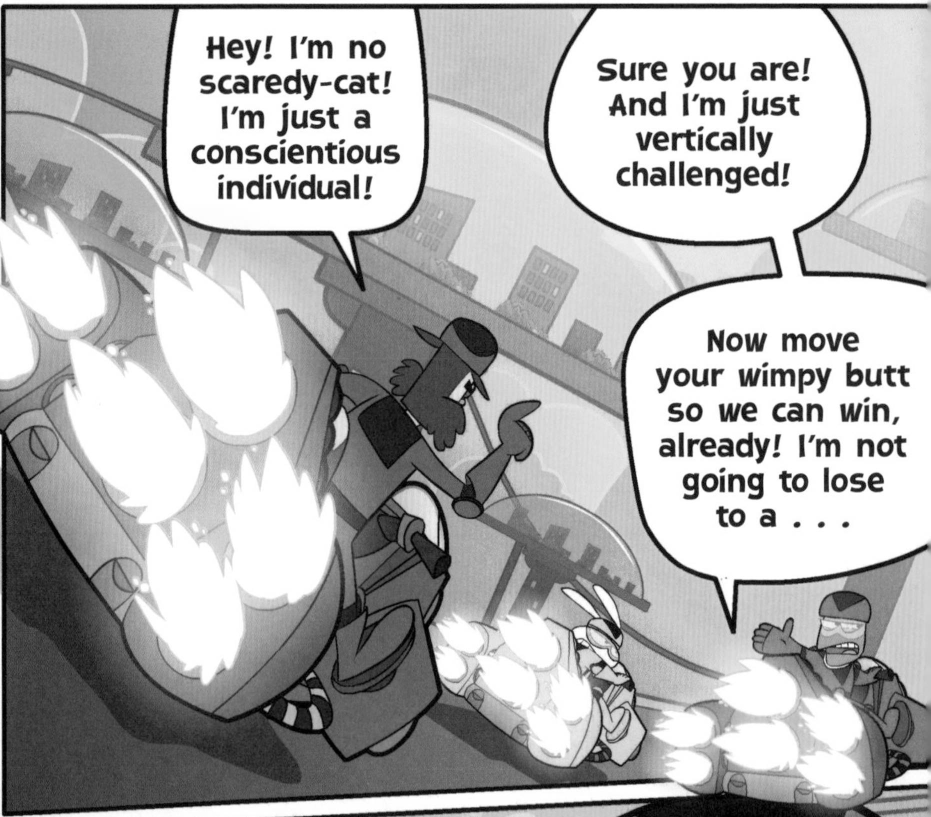
Hey! I'm no scaredy-cat! I'm just a conscientious individual!
Sure you are! And I'm just vertically challenged!
Now move your wimpy butt so we can win, already! I'm not going to lose to a . . .
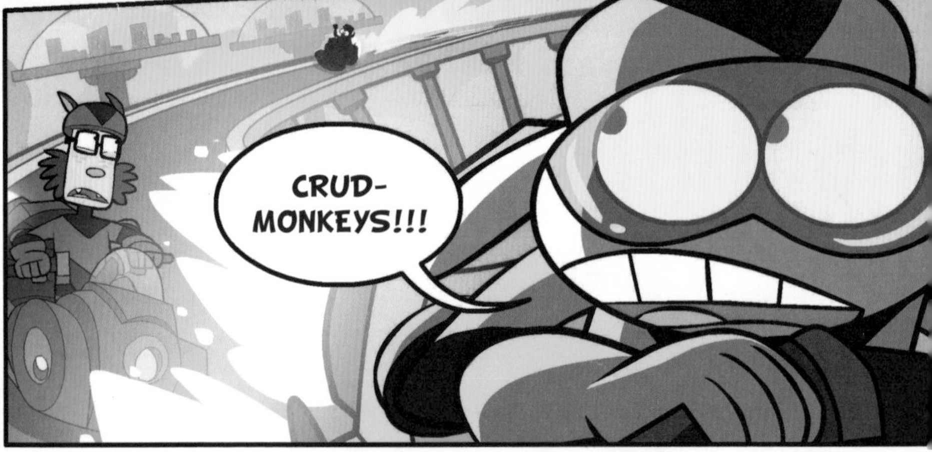
CRUD-MONKEYS!!!

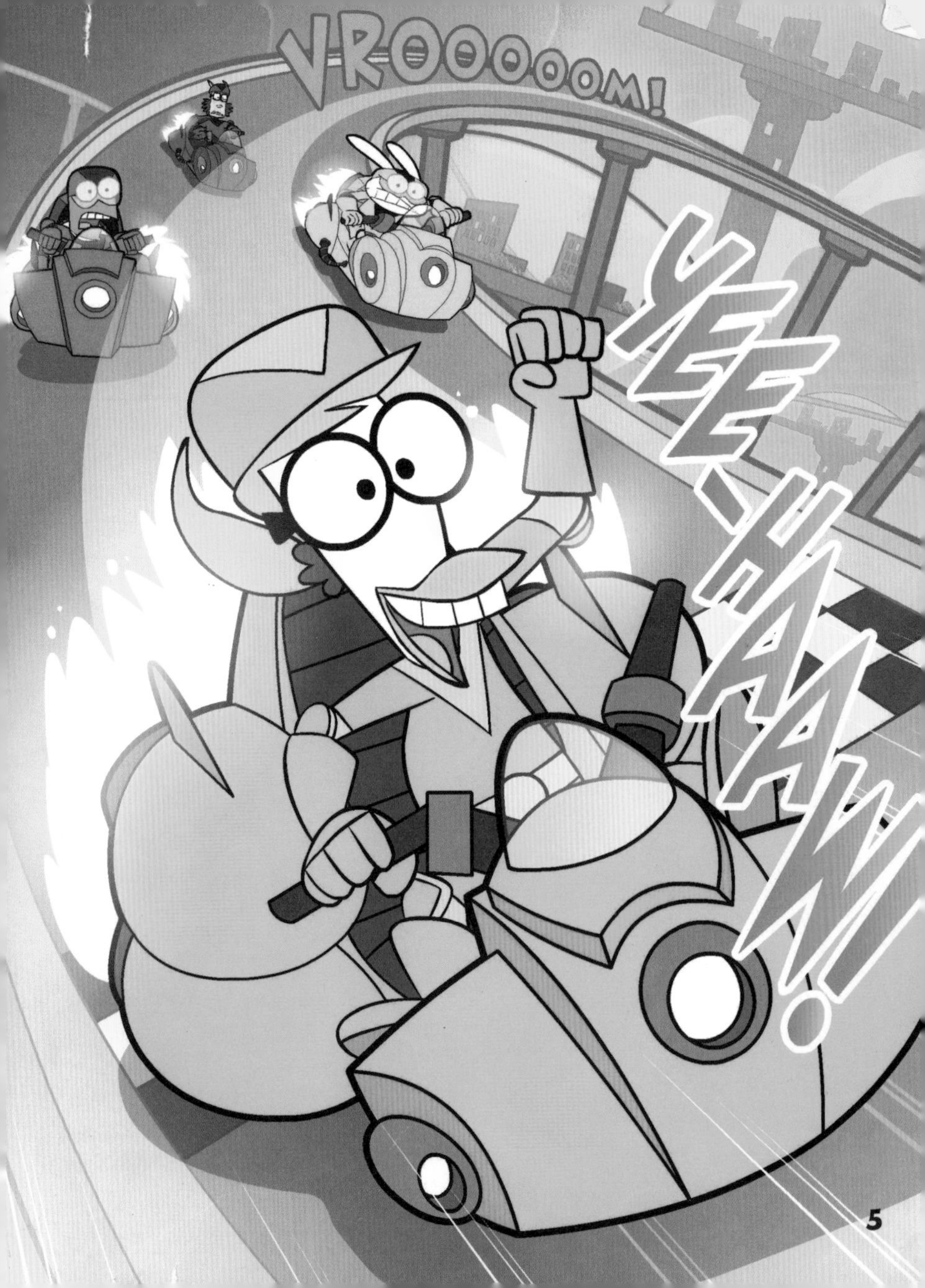
VROOOOOM!
YEE-HAAAW!

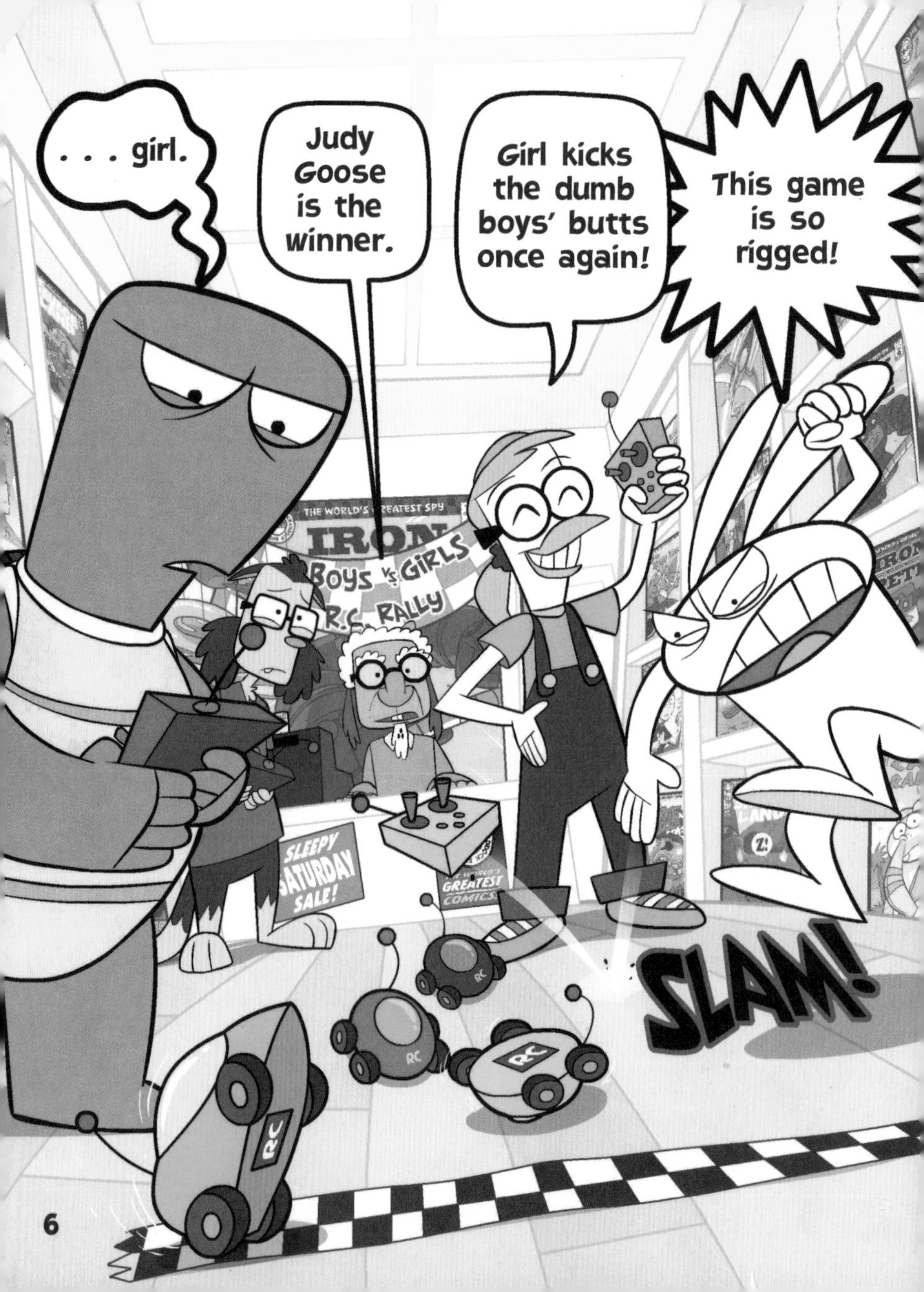

. . . girl.
Judy Goose is the winner.
Girl kicks the dumb boys' butts once again!
This game is so rigged!
THE WORLD'S GREATEST SPY
IRON
BOYS VS. GIRLS R.C. RALLY
SLEEPY SATURDAY SALE!
GREATEST COMICS
SLAM!

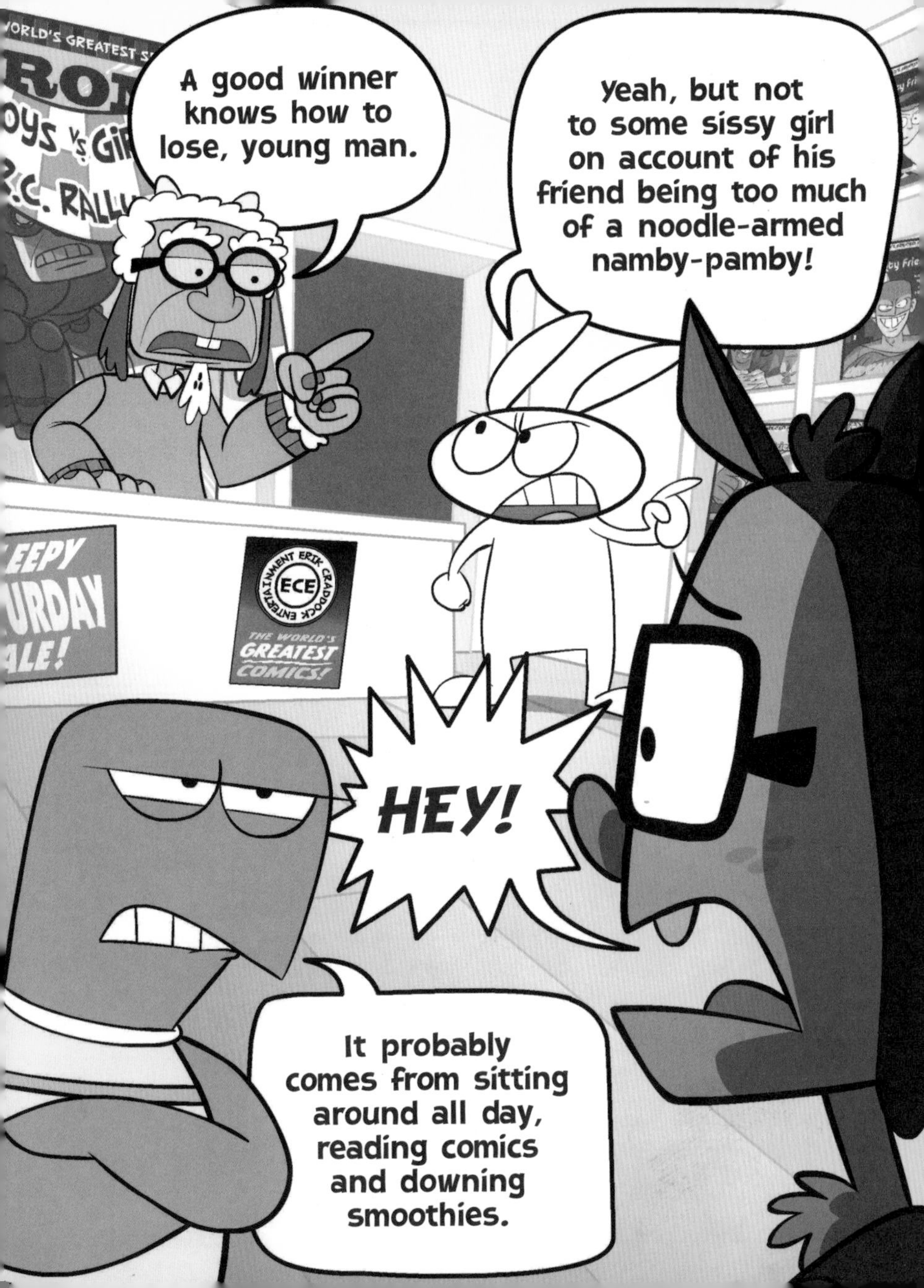
WORLD'S GREATEST S
ROB
OYS VS GIR
R.C. RALLY
A good winner knows how to lose, young man.
Yeah, but not to some sissy girl on account of his friend being too much of a noodle-armed namby-pamby!
EEPY URDAY ALE!
ERIK CRADDOCK ENTERTAINMENT ECE
THE WORLD'S GREATEST COMICS!
HEY!
It probably comes from sitting around all day, reading comics and downing smoothies.

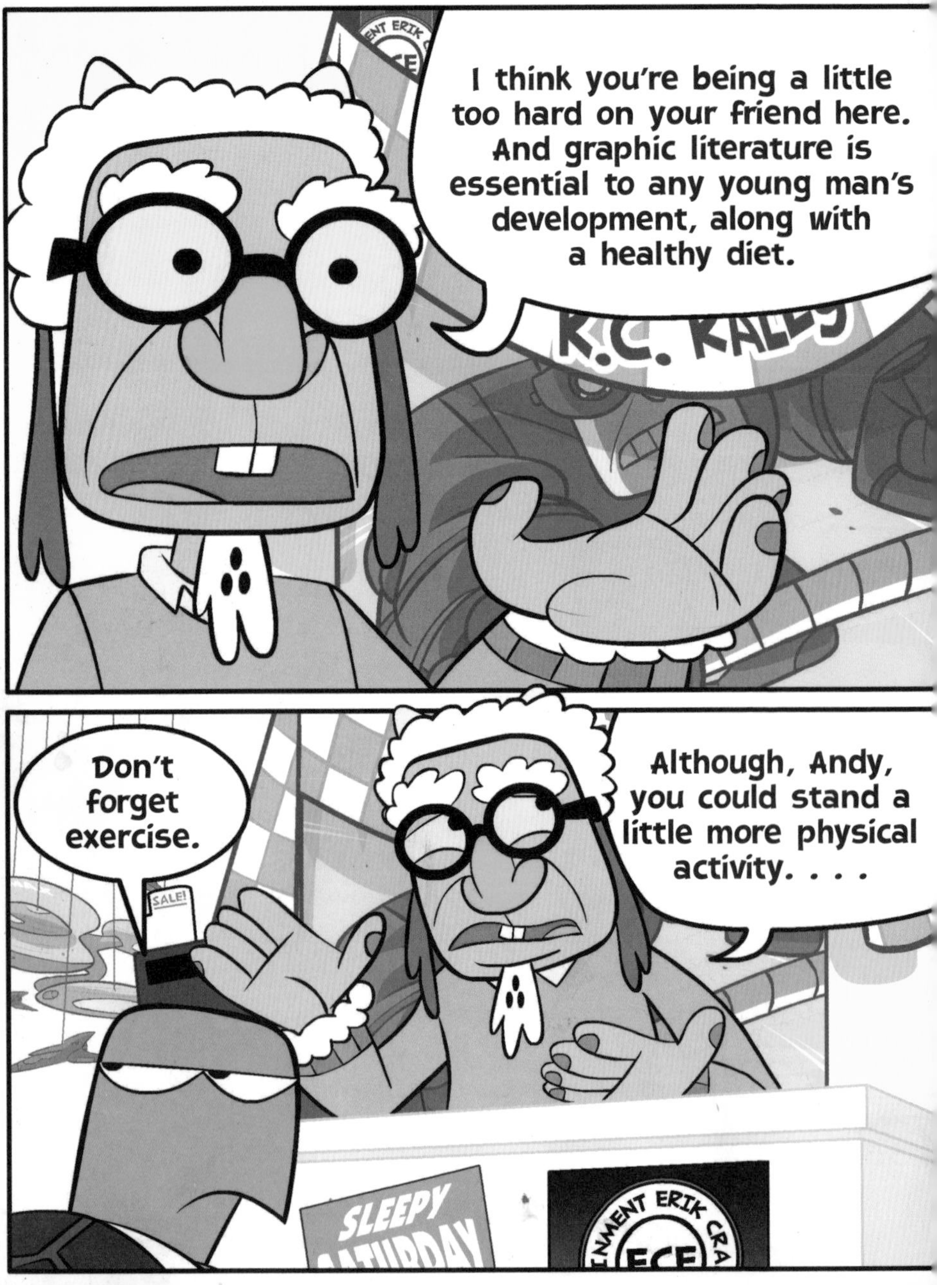
I think you're being a little too hard on your friend here. And graphic literature is essential to any young man's development, along with a healthy diet.
Don't forget exercise.
SALE!
Although, Andy, you could stand a little more physical activity. . . .
SLEEPY

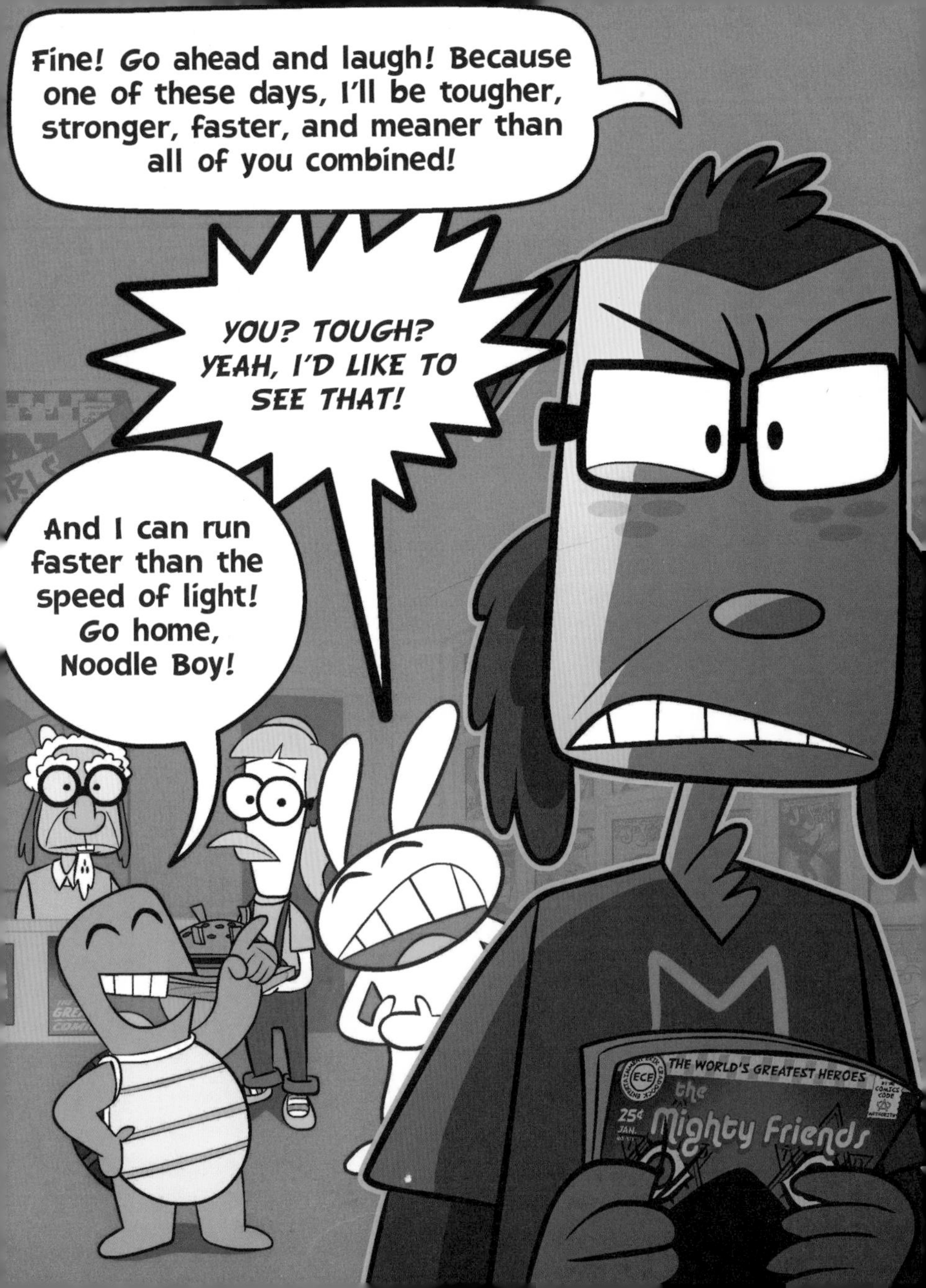
Fine! Go ahead and laugh! Because one of these days, I'll be tougher, stronger, faster, and meaner than all of you combined!
YOU? TOUGH? YEAH, I'D LIKE TO SEE THAT!
And I can run faster than the speed of light! Go home, Noodle Boy!
THE WORLD'S GREATEST HEROES
the Mighty Friends
25¢

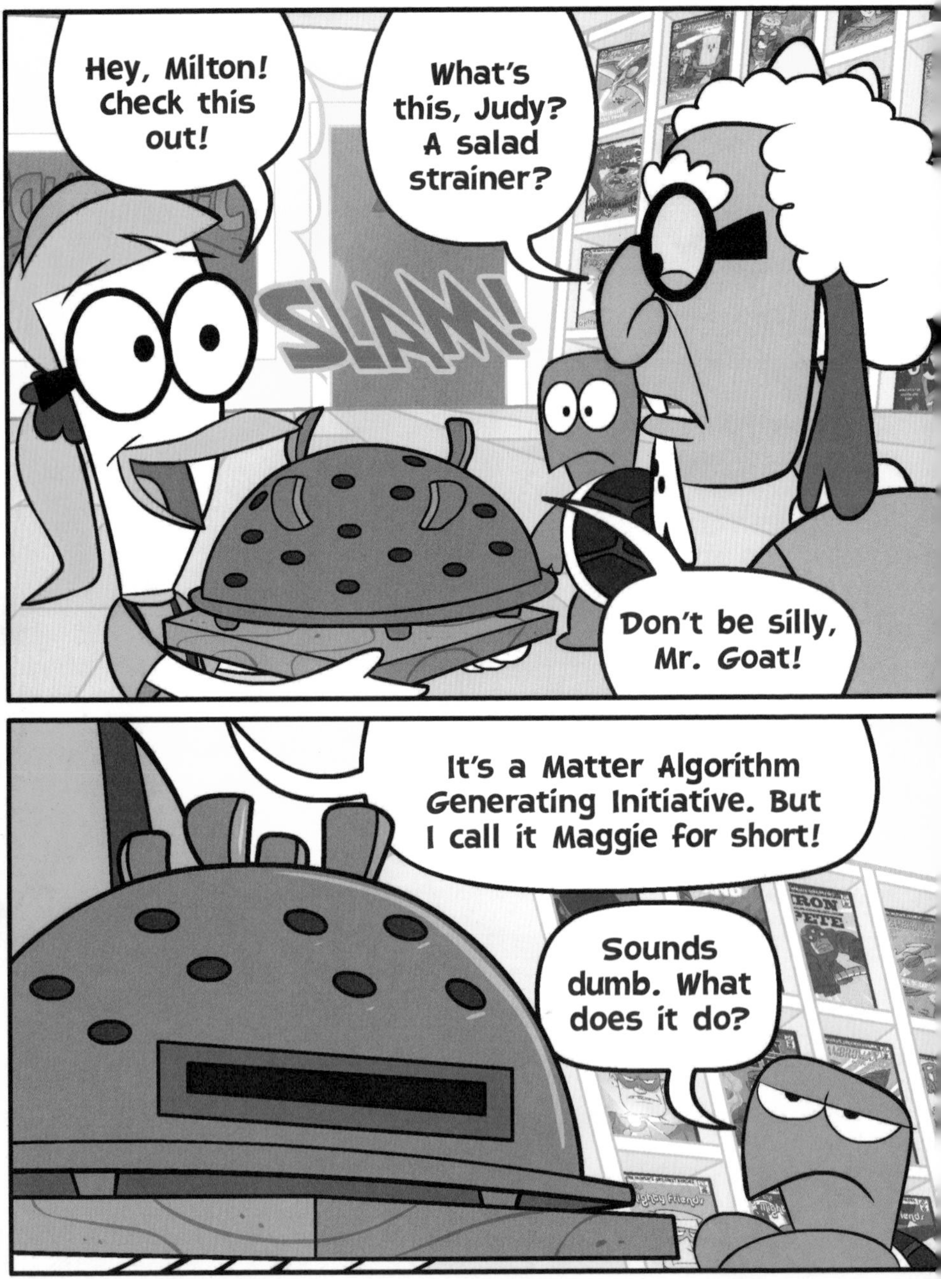
Hey, Milton! Check this out!
What's this, Judy? A salad strainer?
SLAM!
Don't be silly, Mr. Goat!
It's a Matter Algorithm Generating Initiative. But I call it Maggie for short!
Sounds dumb. What does it do?
IRON PETE

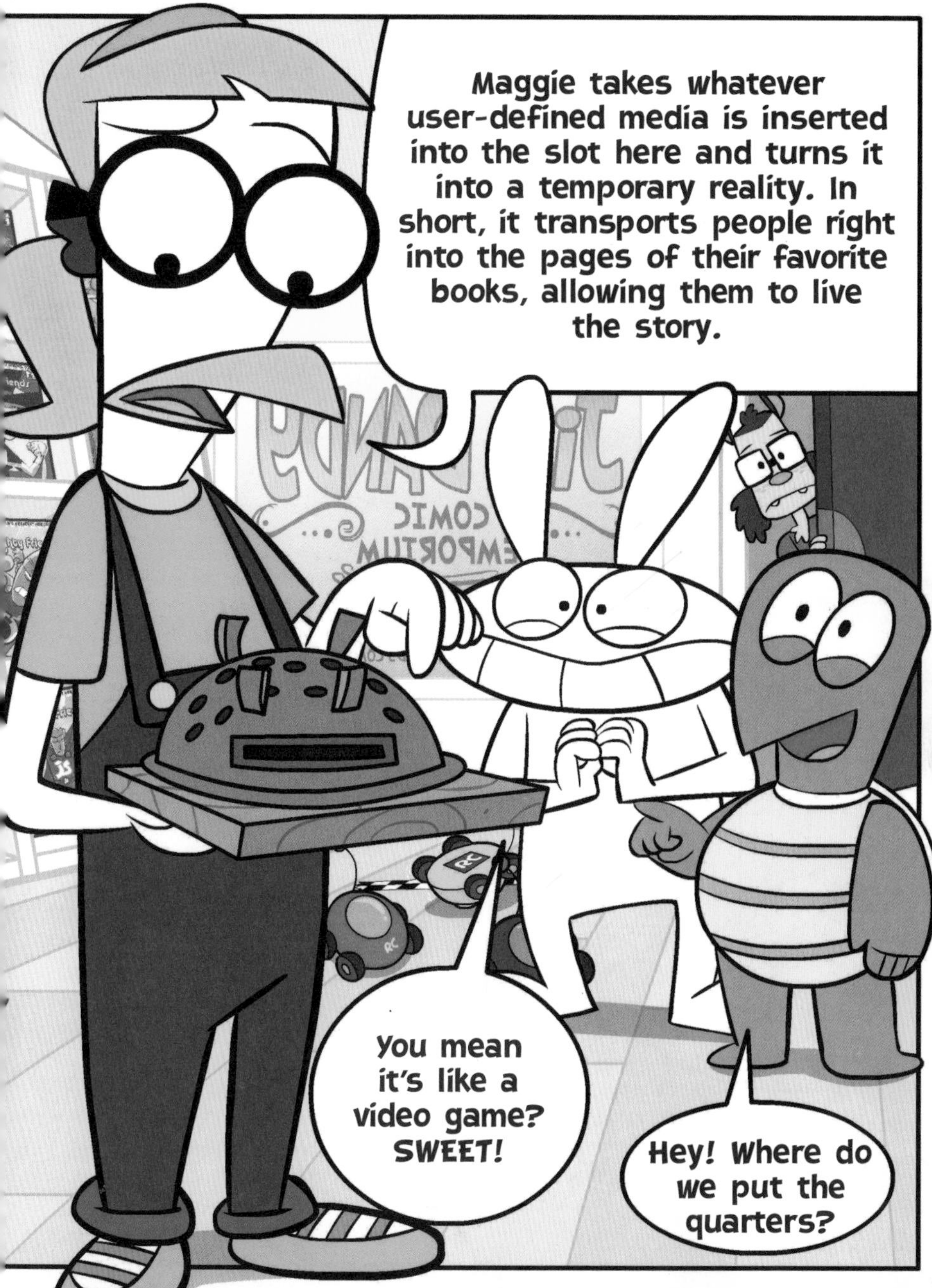
Maggie takes whatever user-defined media is inserted into the slot here and turns it into a temporary reality. In short, it transports people right into the pages of their favorite books, allowing them to live the story.
You mean it's like a video game? SWEET!
Hey! Where do we put the quarters?

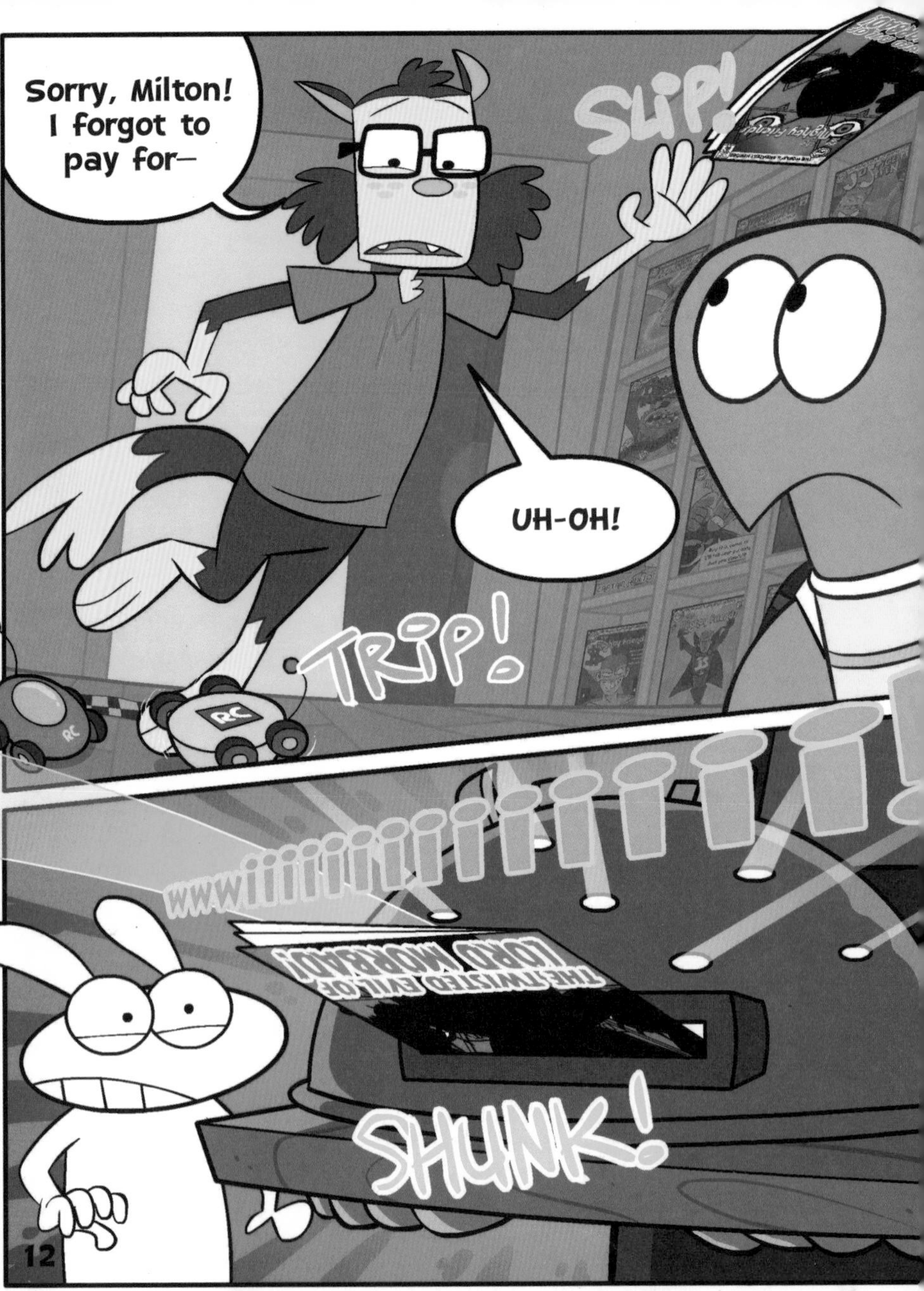
Sorry, Milton! I forgot to pay for–
SLIP!
UH-OH!
TRIP!
WWWIIIIIIIIIIIII!
THE TWISTED EVIL OF LORD MORBAD!
SHUNK!

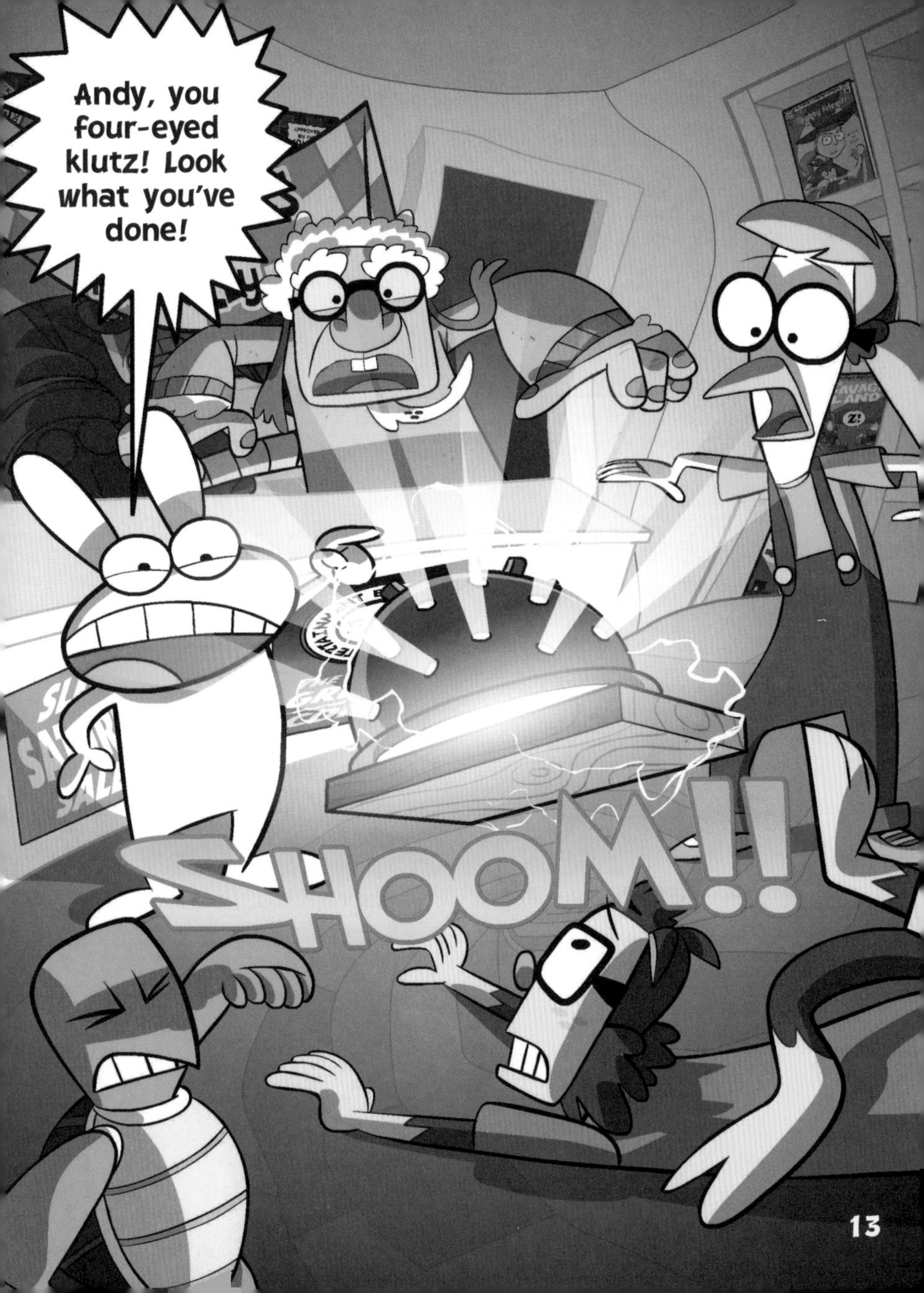
Andy, you four-eyed klutz! Look what you've done!
SHOOM!!

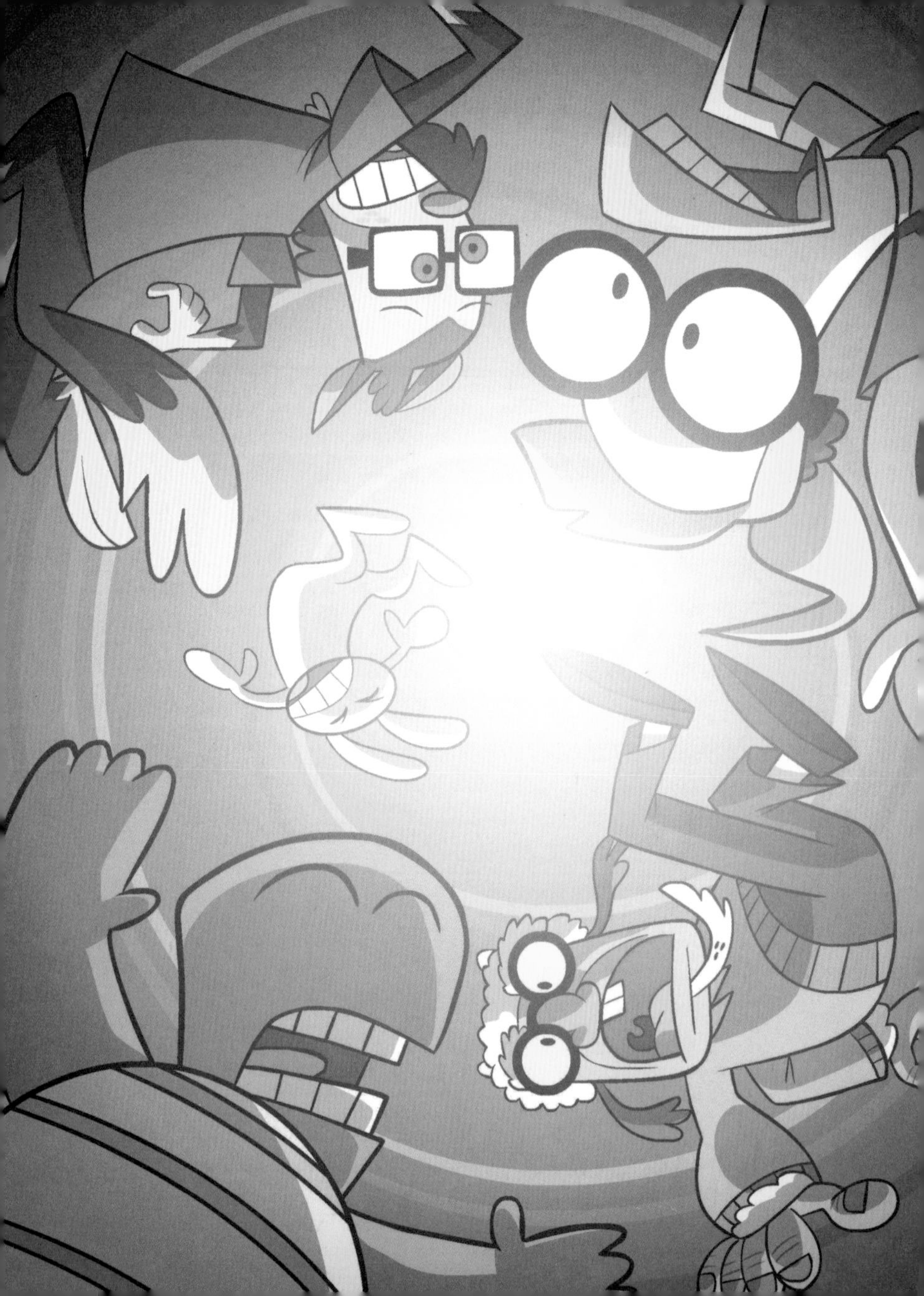

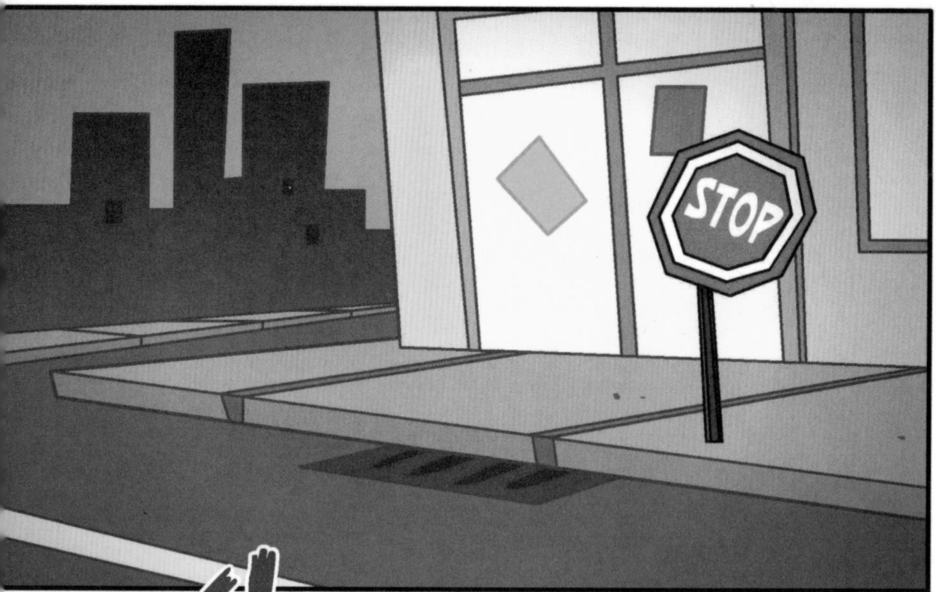
STOP

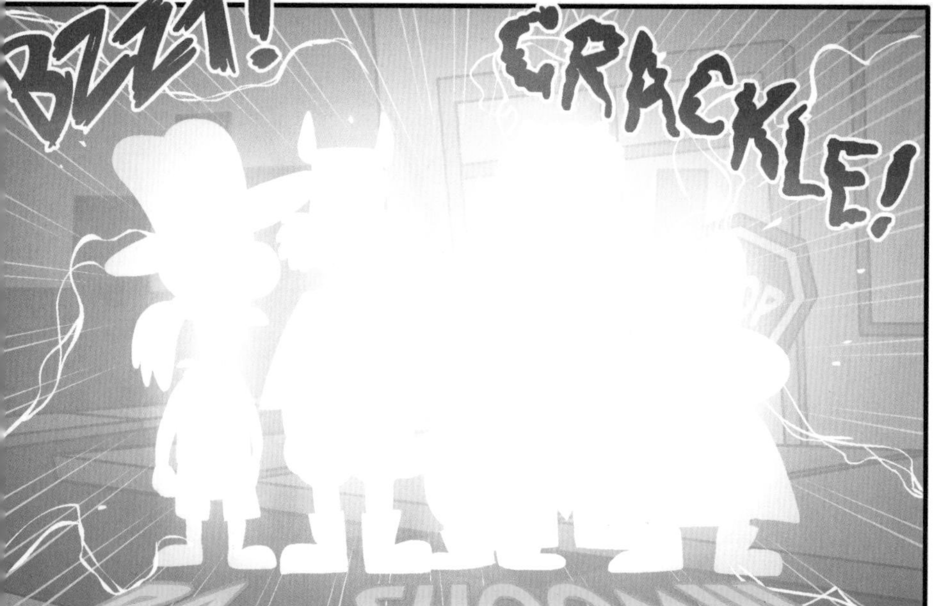
BZZZT!
CRACKLE!
BA - SHOOM!!!...

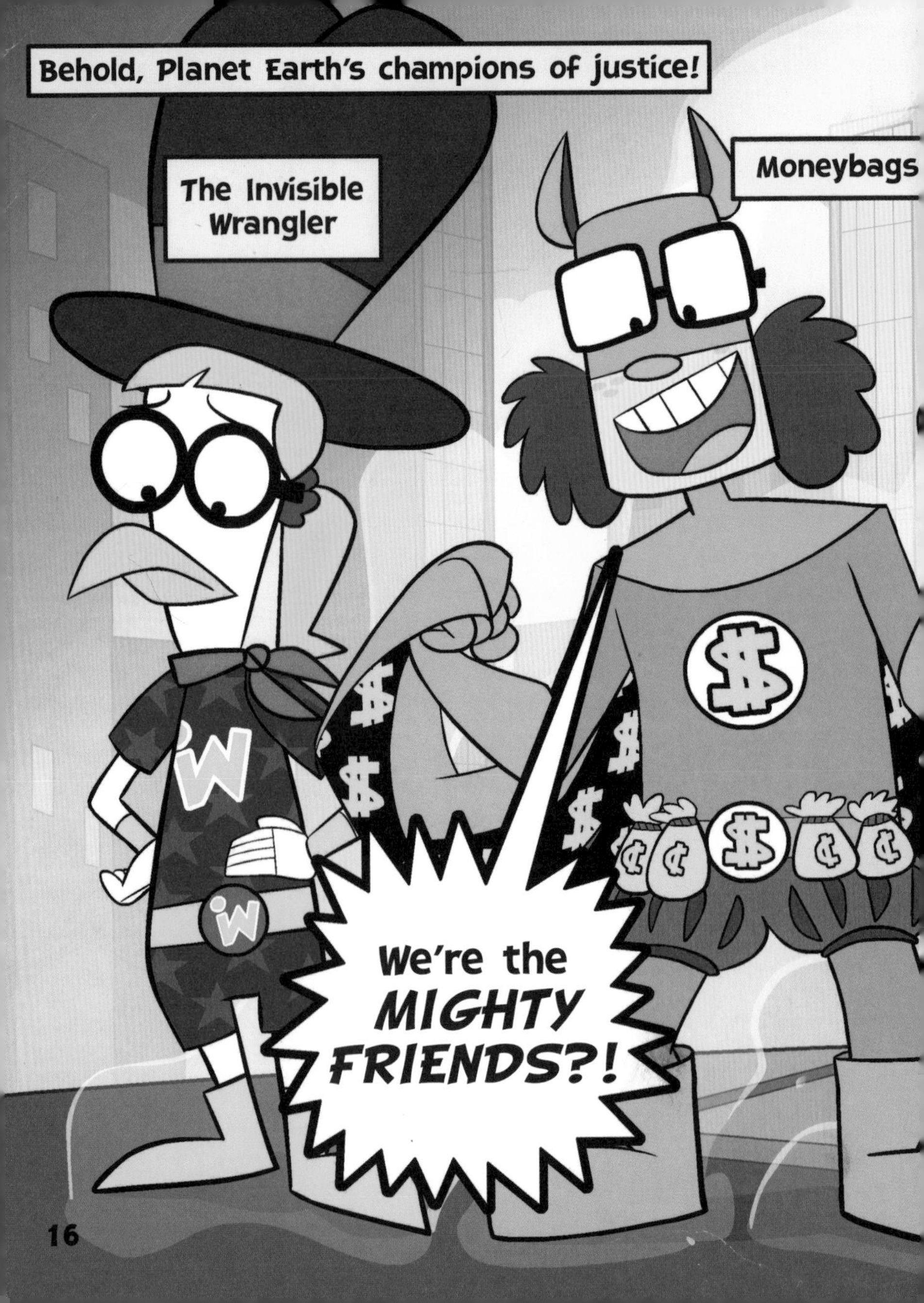
Behold, Planet Earth's champions of justice!
The Invisible Wrangler
Moneybags
We're the *MIGHTY FRIENDS?!*

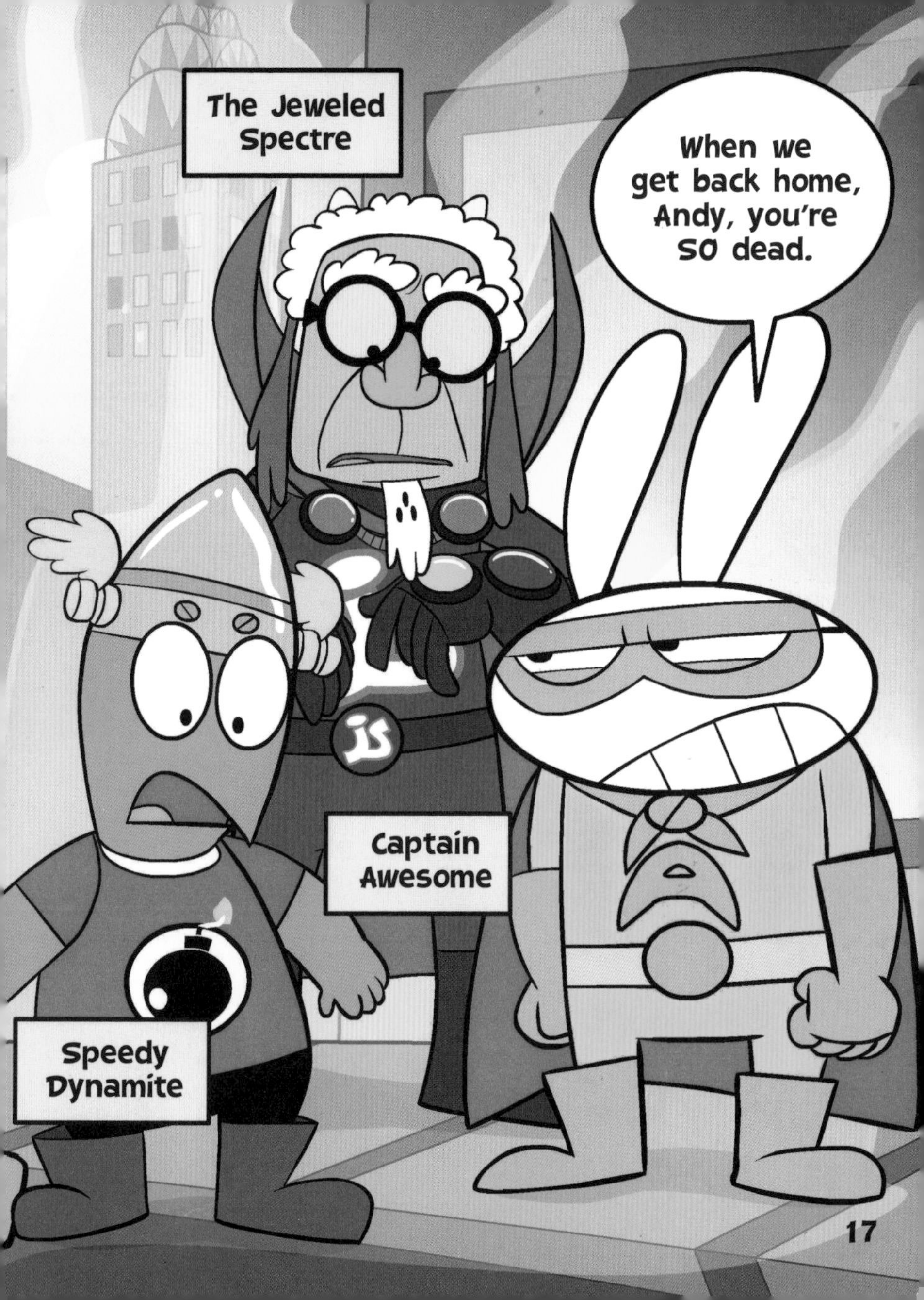
The Jeweled Spectre
When we get back home, Andy, you're SO dead.
Captain Awesome
Speedy Dynamite

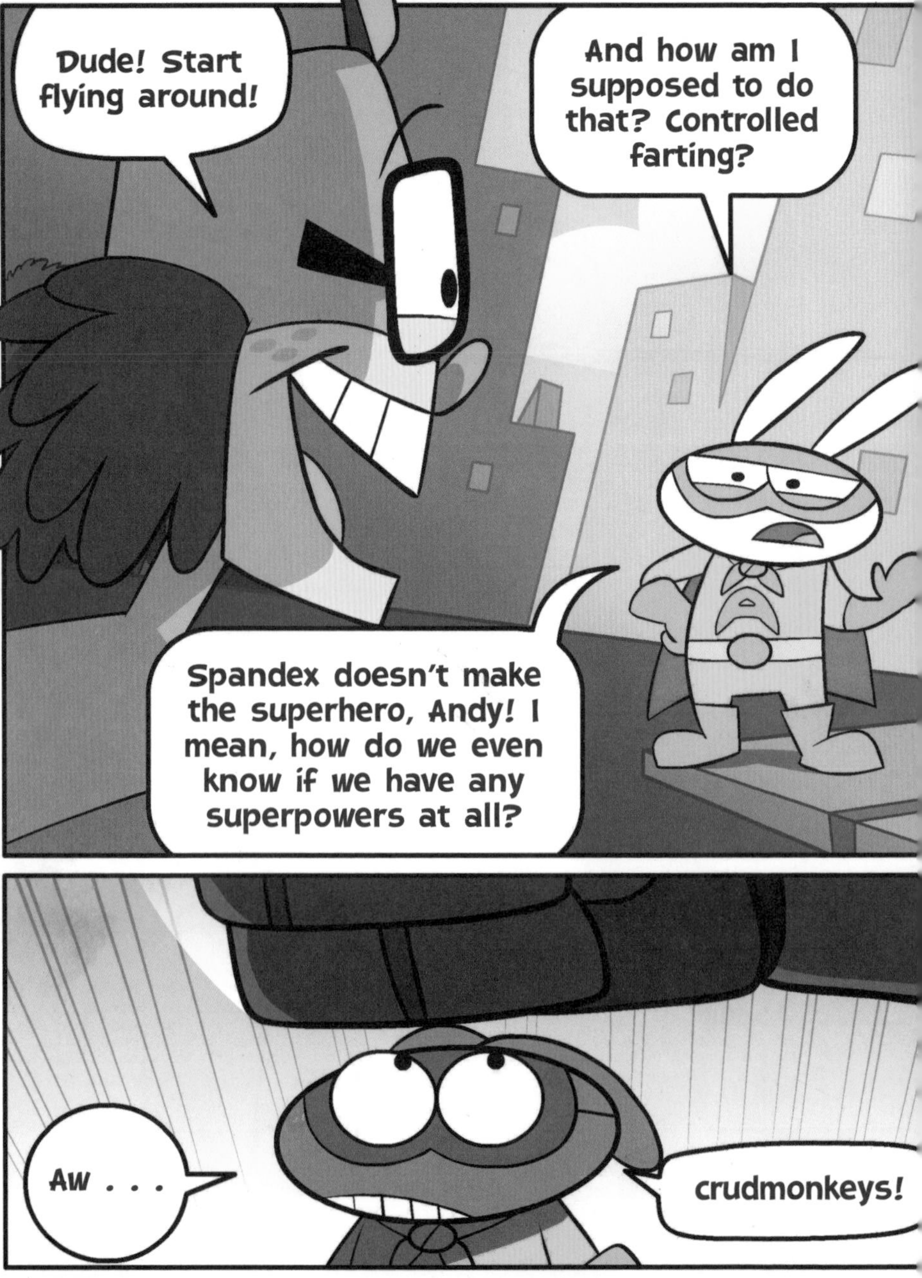
Dude! Start flying around!
And how am I supposed to do that? Controlled farting?
Spandex doesn't make the superhero, Andy! I mean, how do we even know if we have any superpowers at all?
Aw . . .
crudmonkeys!

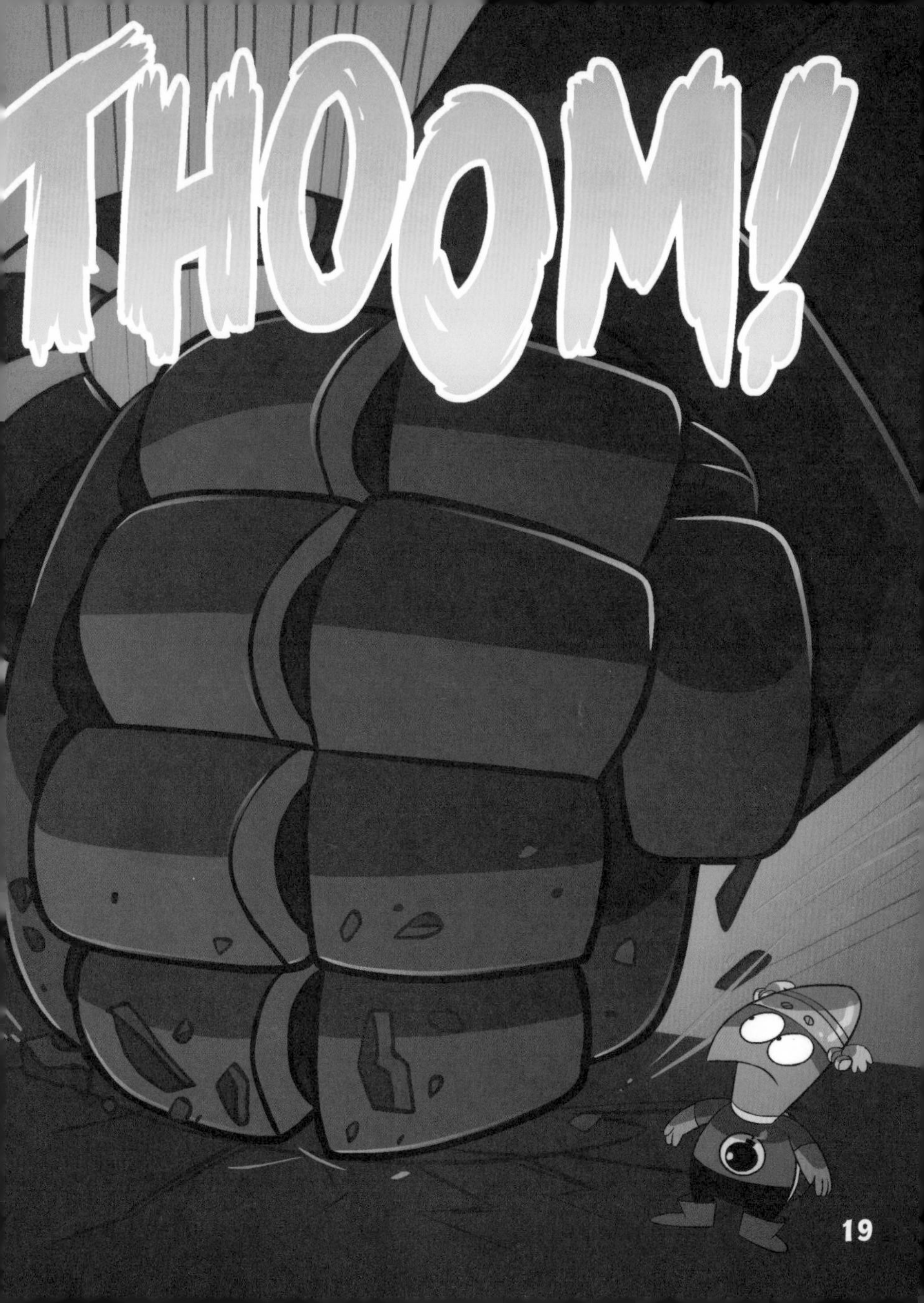
THOOM!

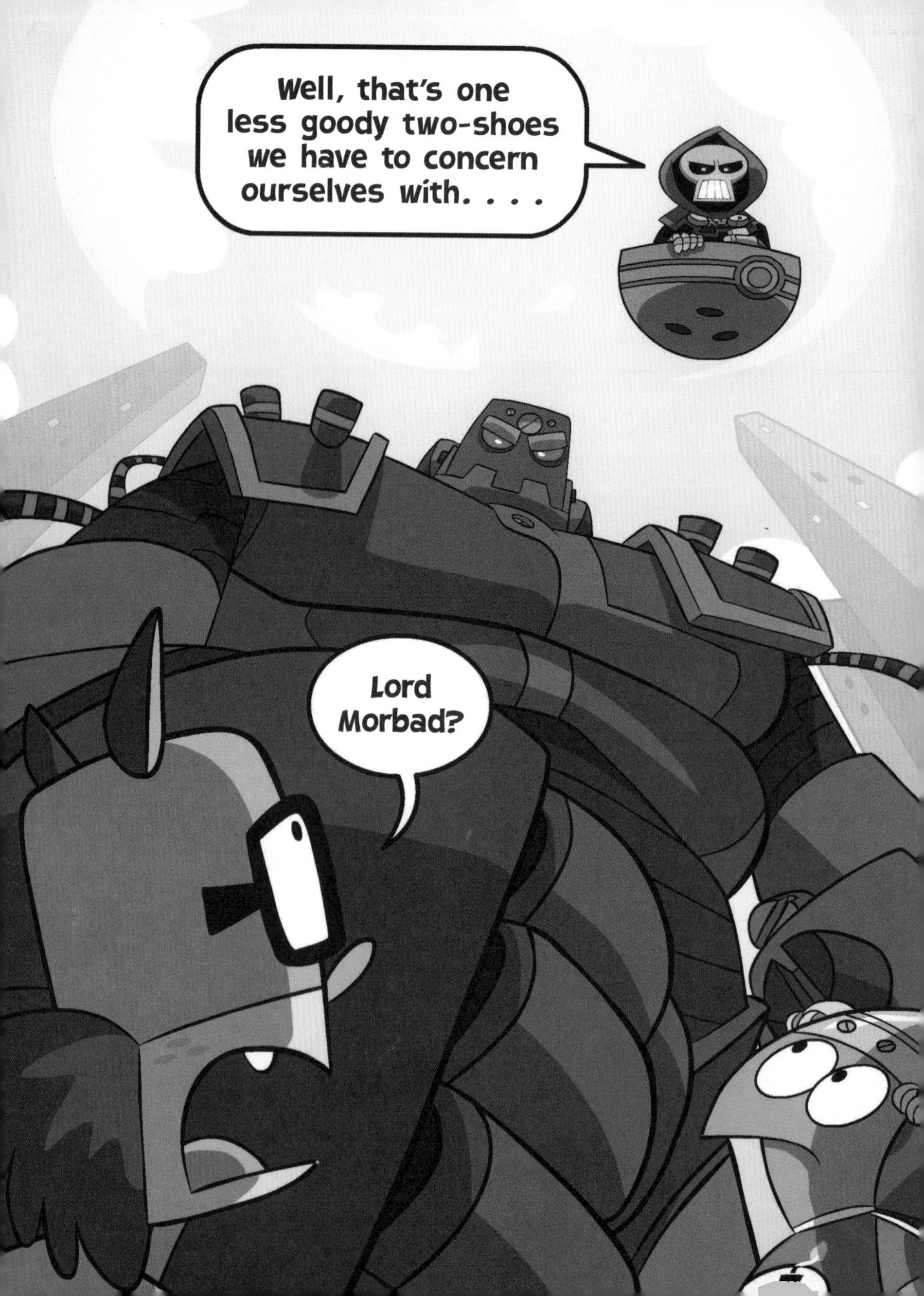
Well, that's one less goody two-shoes we have to concern ourselves with. . . .
Lord Morbad?

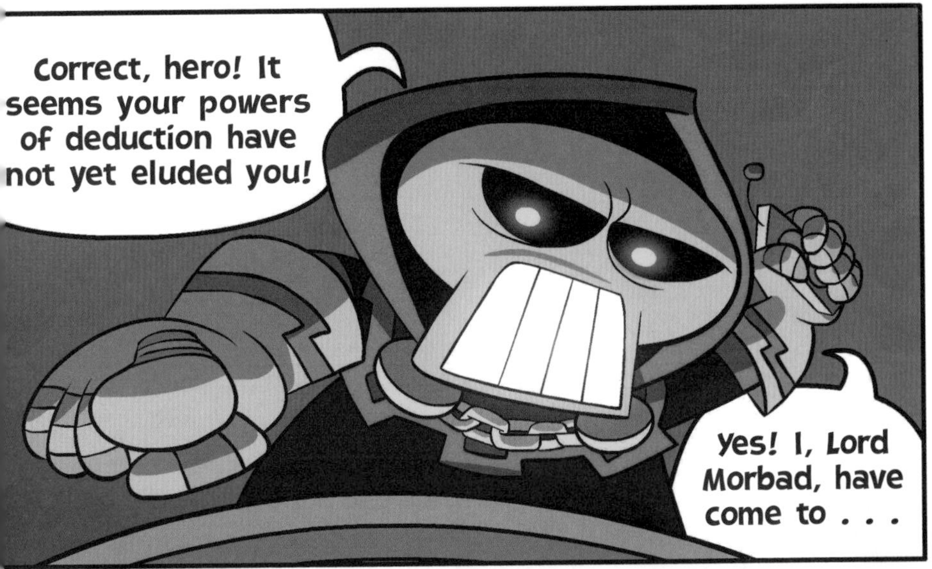
Correct, hero! It seems your powers of deduction have not yet eluded you!
Yes! I, Lord Morbad, have come to . . .

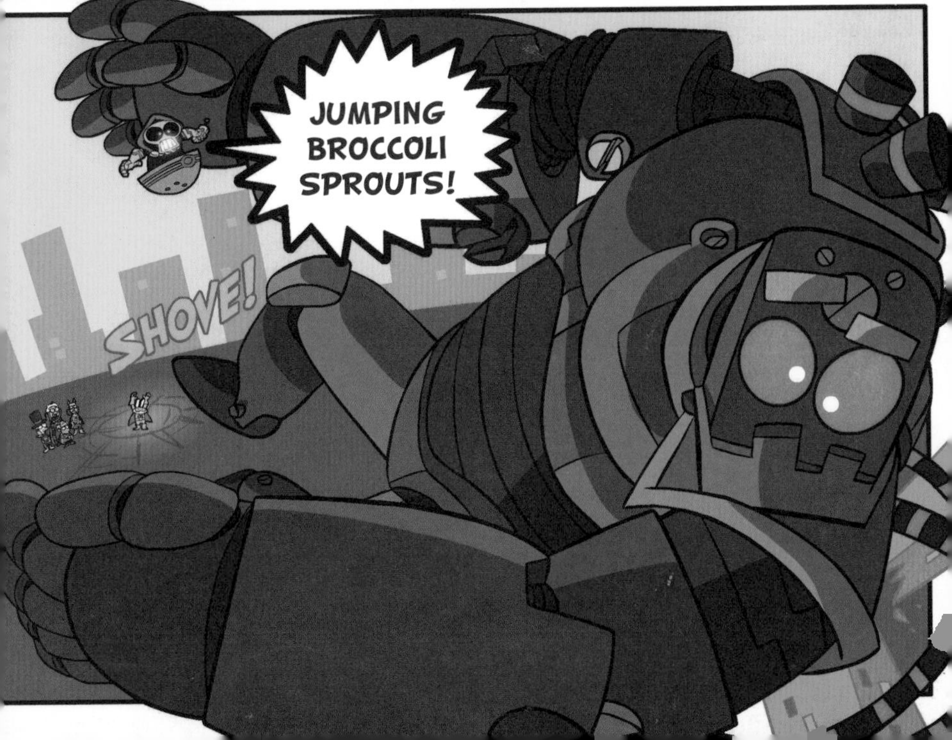
JUMPING BROCCOLI SPROUTS!
SHOVE!

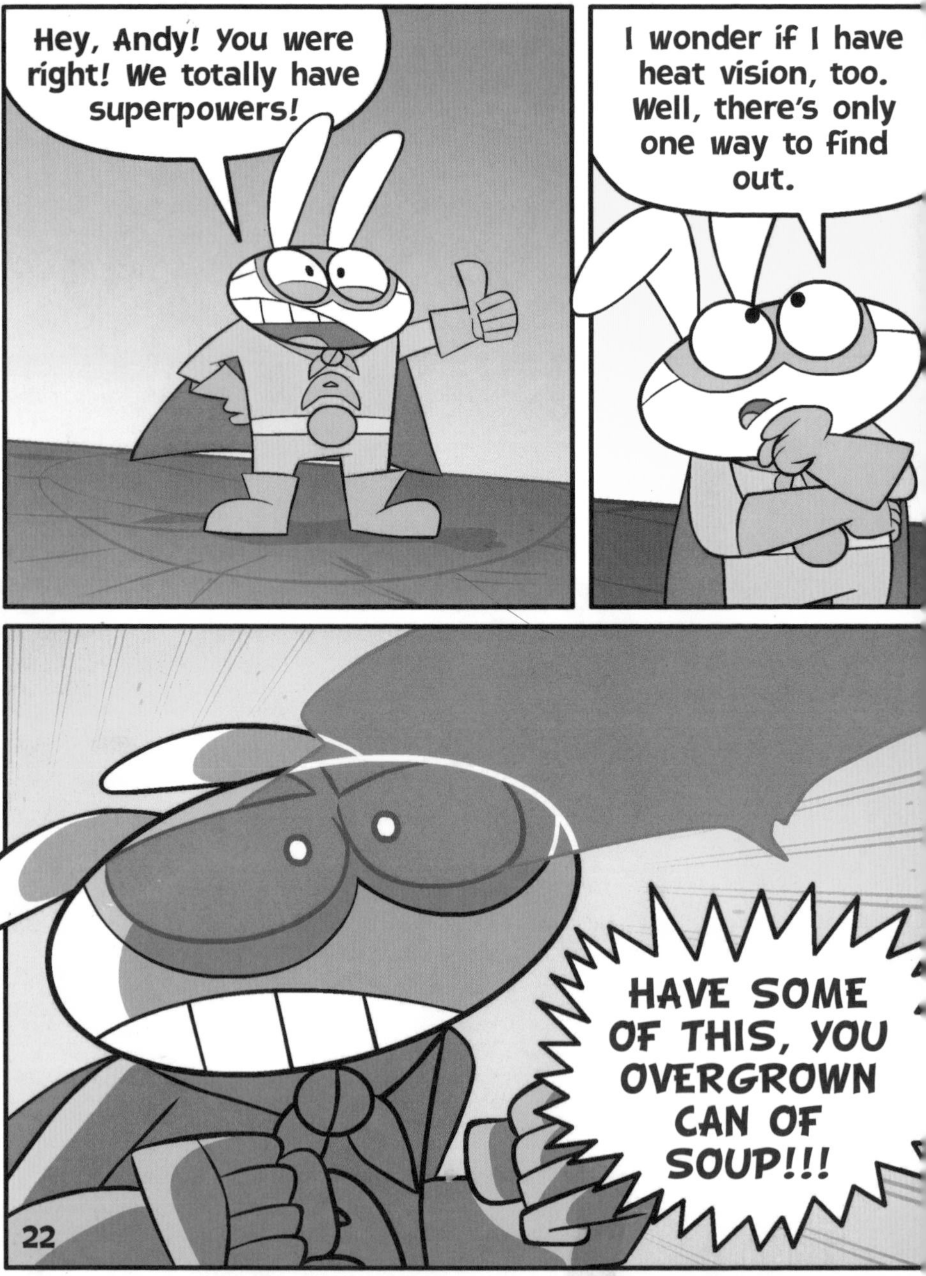
Hey, Andy! You were right! We totally have superpowers!
I wonder if I have heat vision, too. Well, there's only one way to find out.
HAVE SOME OF THIS, YOU OVERGROWN CAN OF SOUP!!!

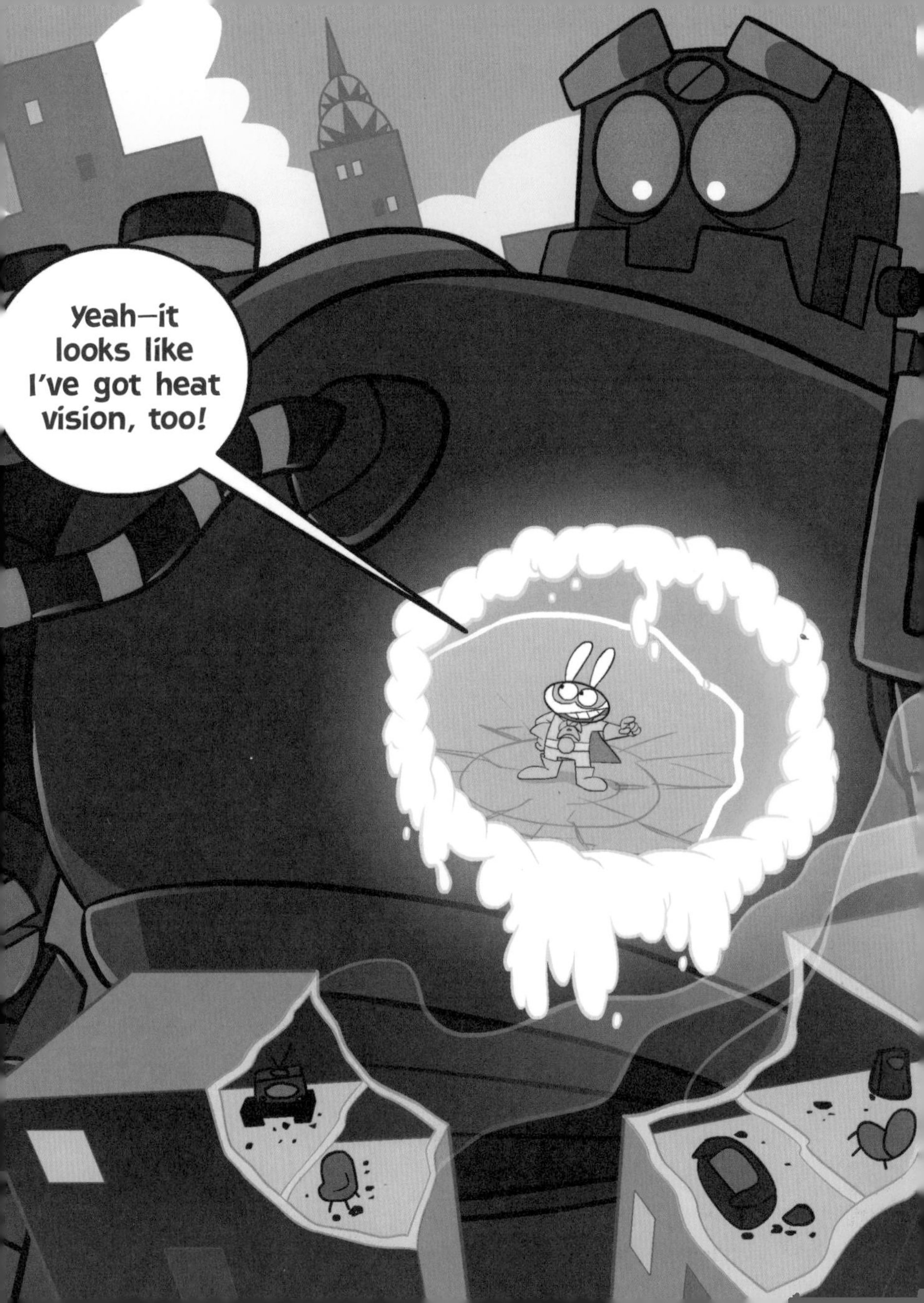
Yeah—it looks like I've got heat vision, too!

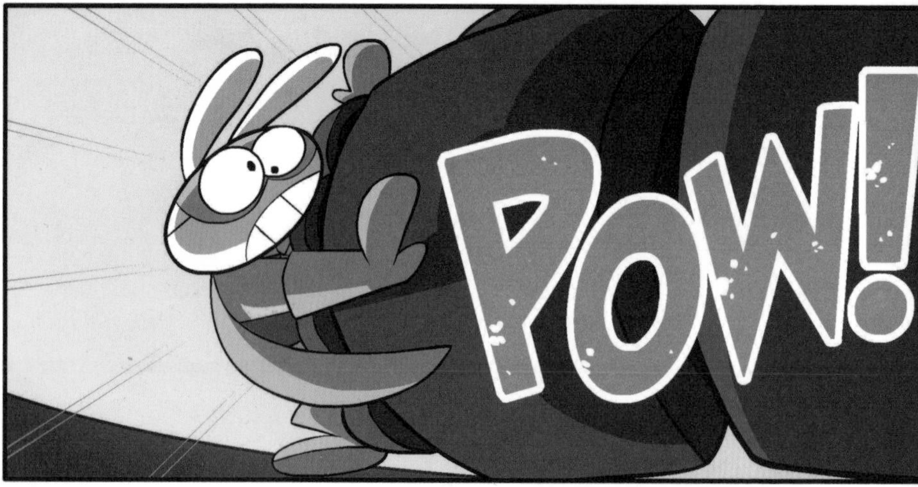
POW!

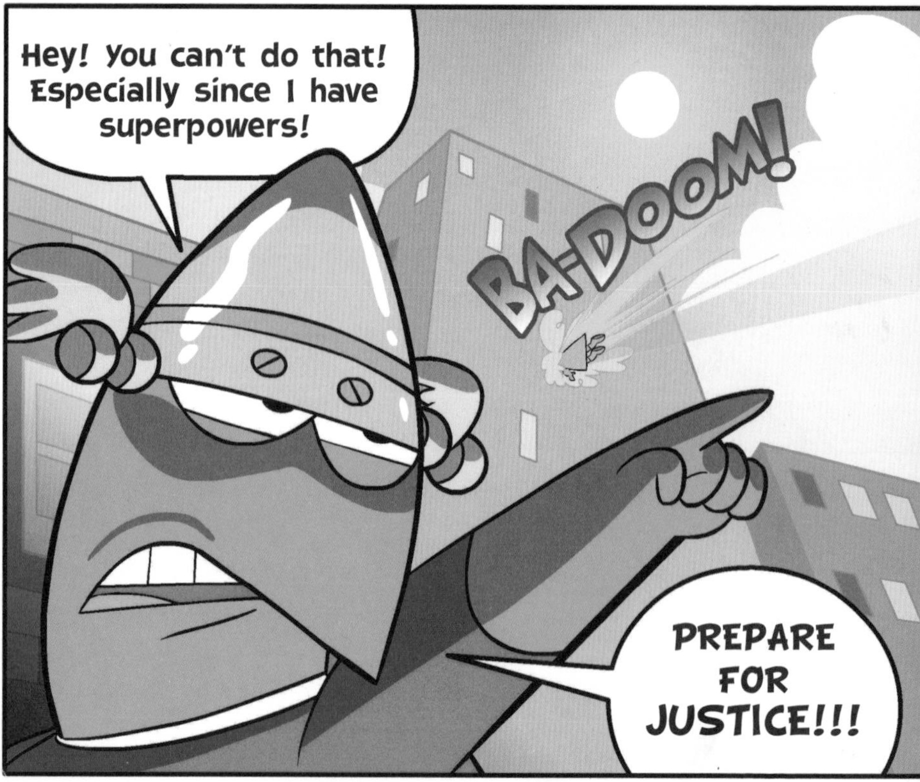
Hey! You can't do that! Especially since I have superpowers!
BA-DOOM!
PREPARE FOR JUSTICE!!!

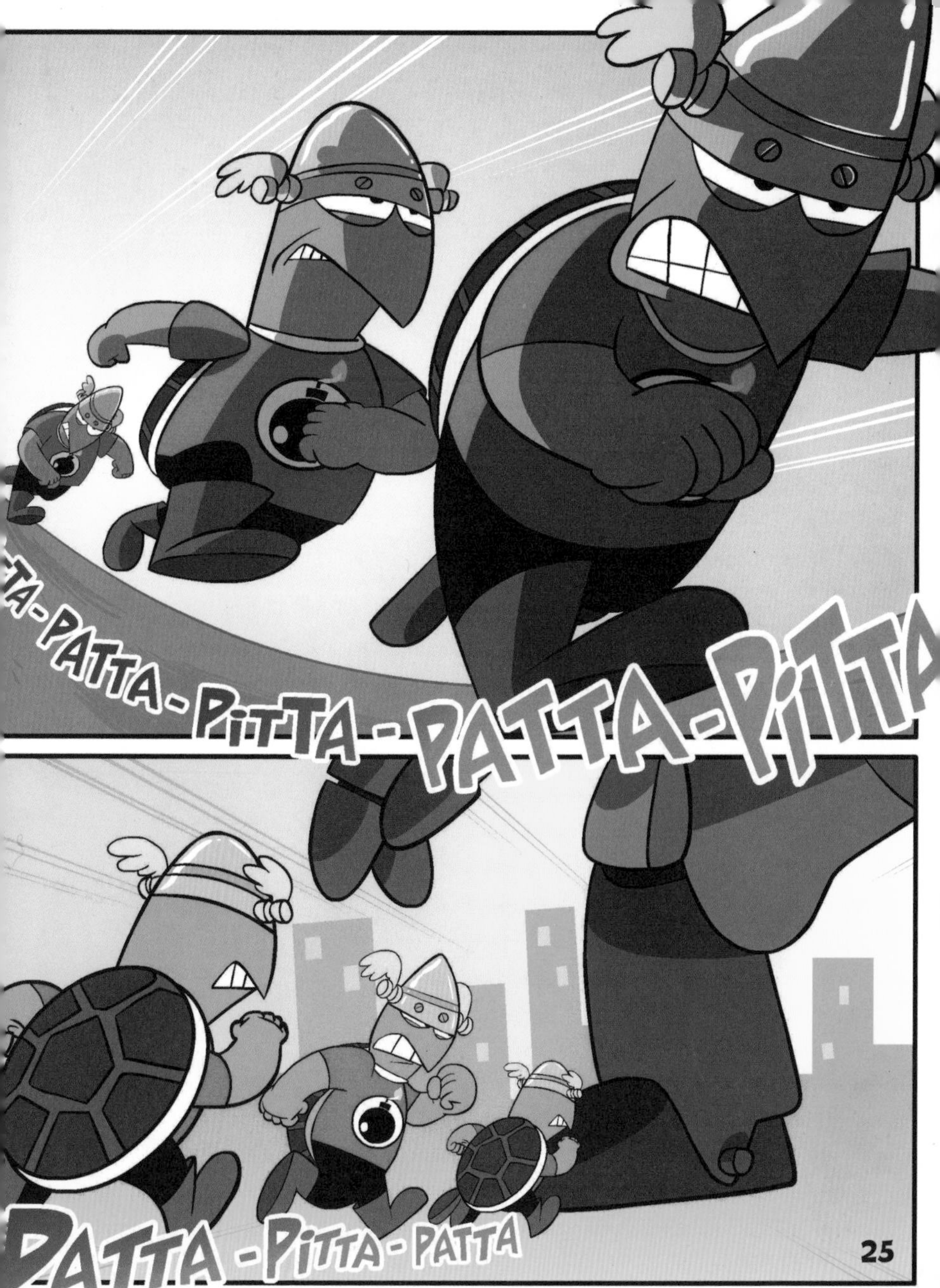
TA-PATTA-PITTA-PATTA-PITTA
PATTA-PITTA-PATTA

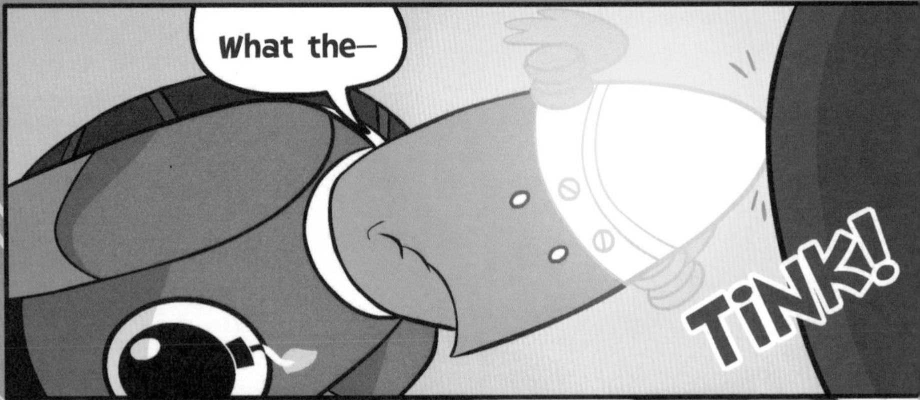
What the—
TiNK!
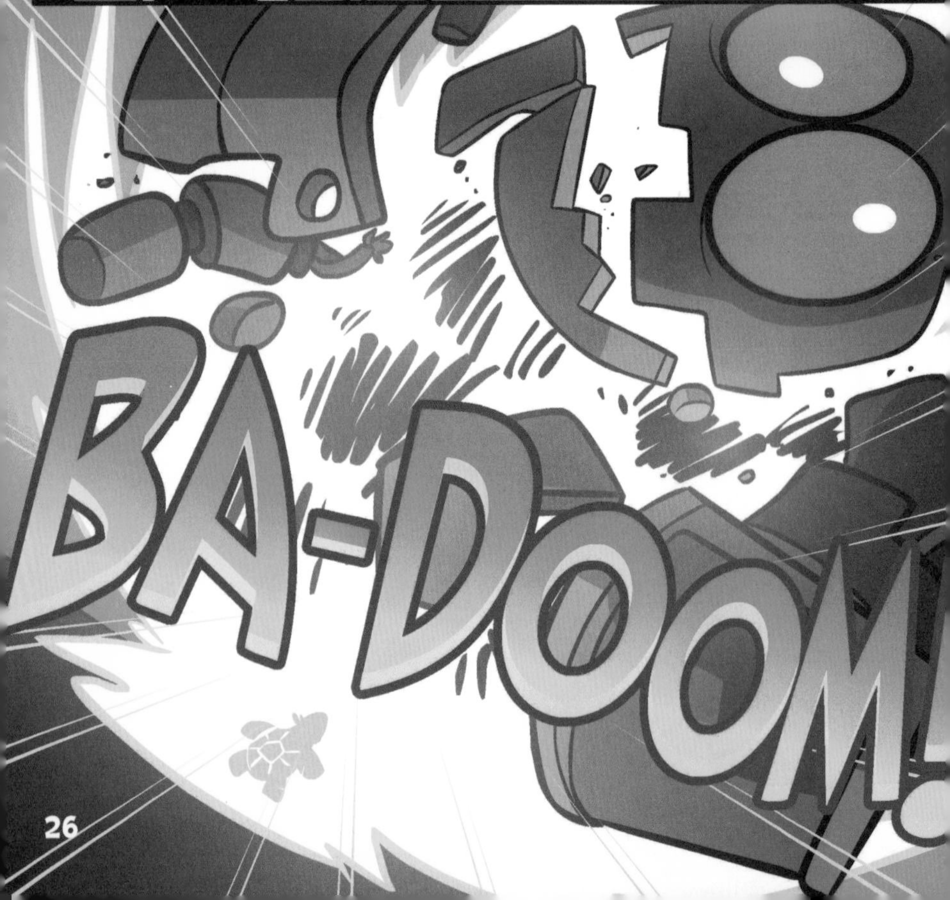
BA-DOOM!

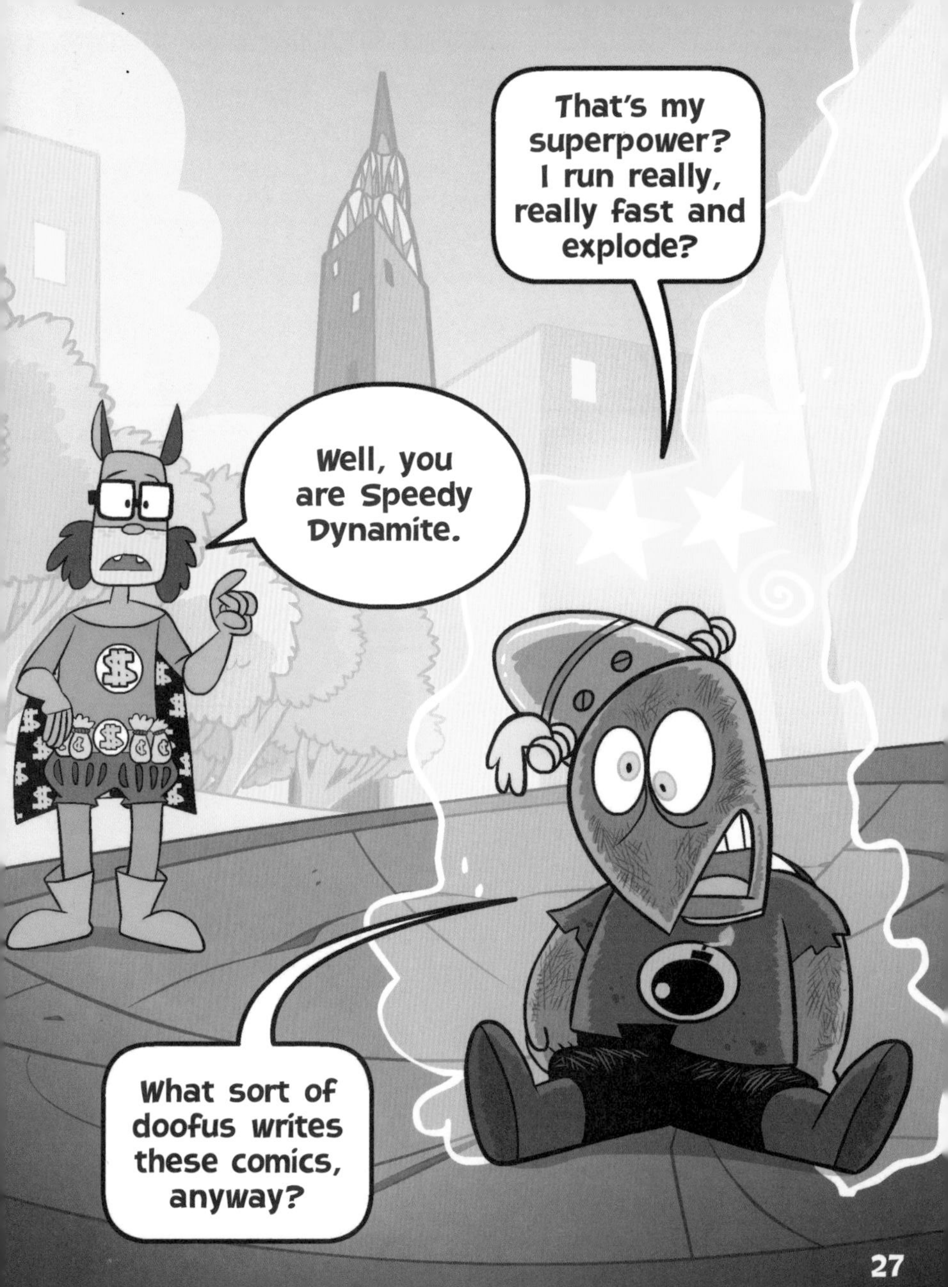
Well, you are Speedy Dynamite.
That's my superpower? I run really, really fast and explode?
What sort of doofus writes these comics, anyway?

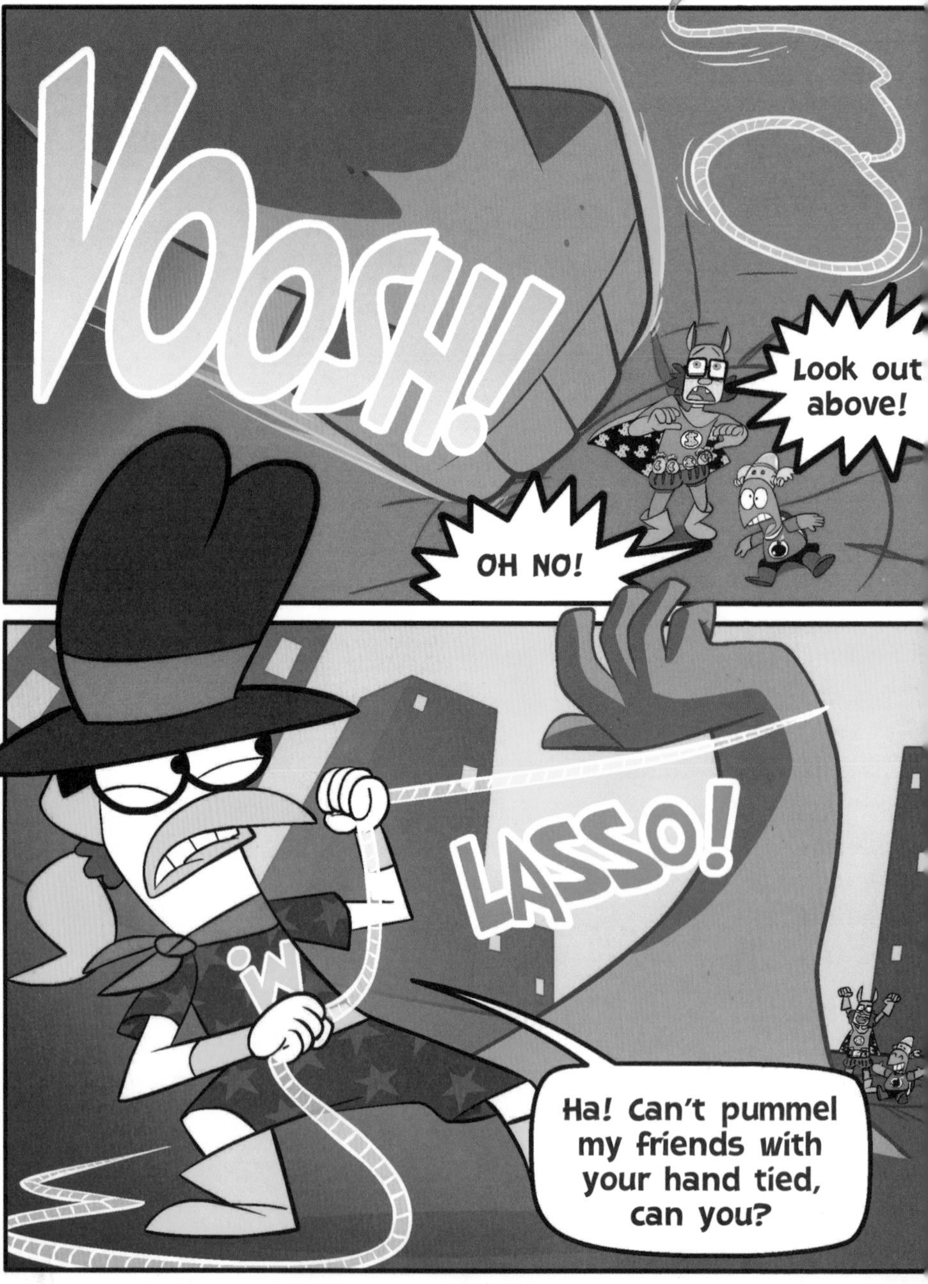
VOOSH!!
Look out above!
OH NO!
LASSO!
Ha! Can't pummel my friends with your hand tied, can you?

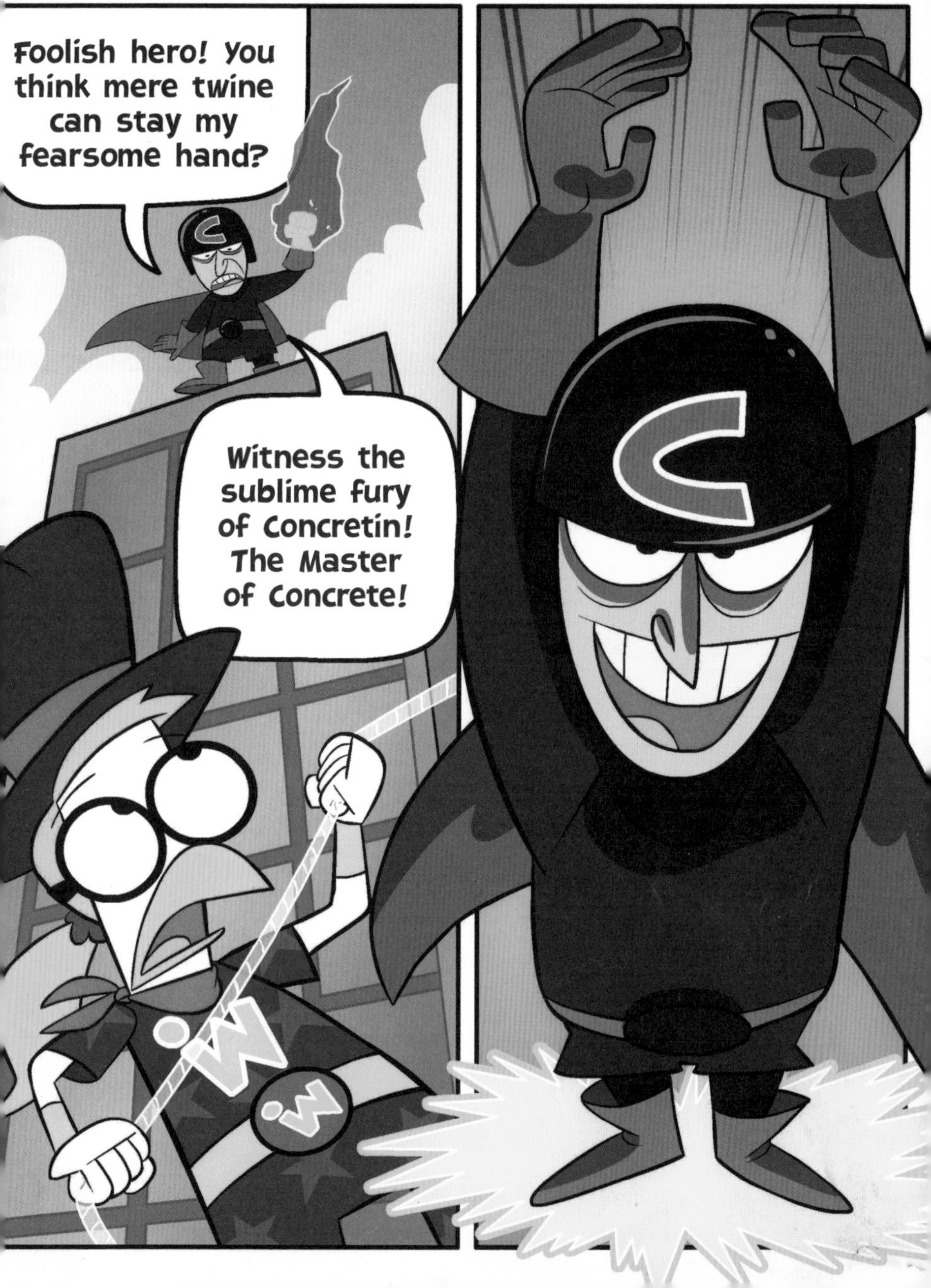

Foolish hero! You think mere twine can stay my fearsome hand?
Witness the sublime fury of Concretin! The Master of Concrete!

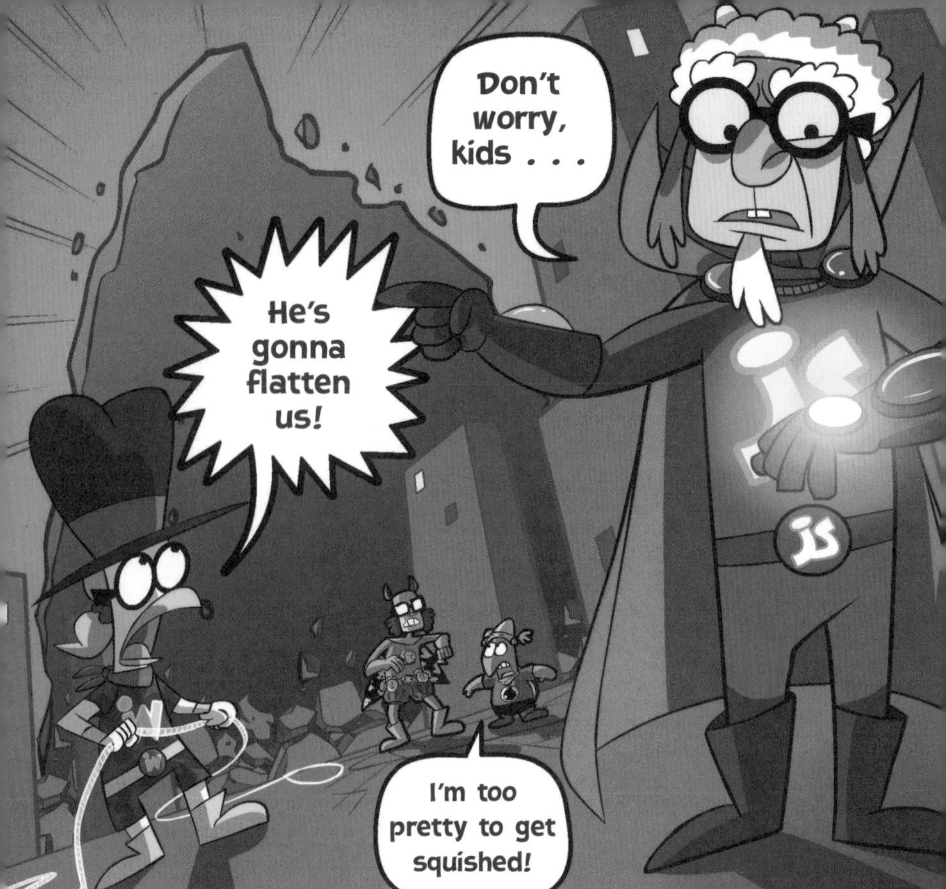
He's gonna flatten us!
Don't worry, kids . . .
I'm too pretty to get squished!
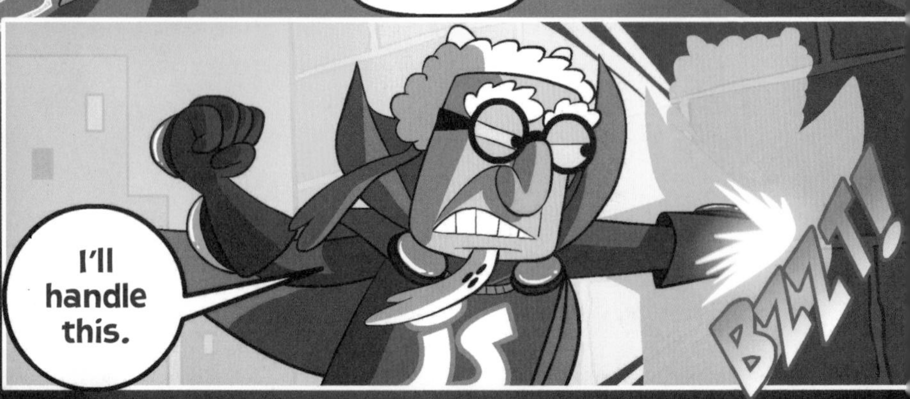
I'll handle this.
BZZZT!!

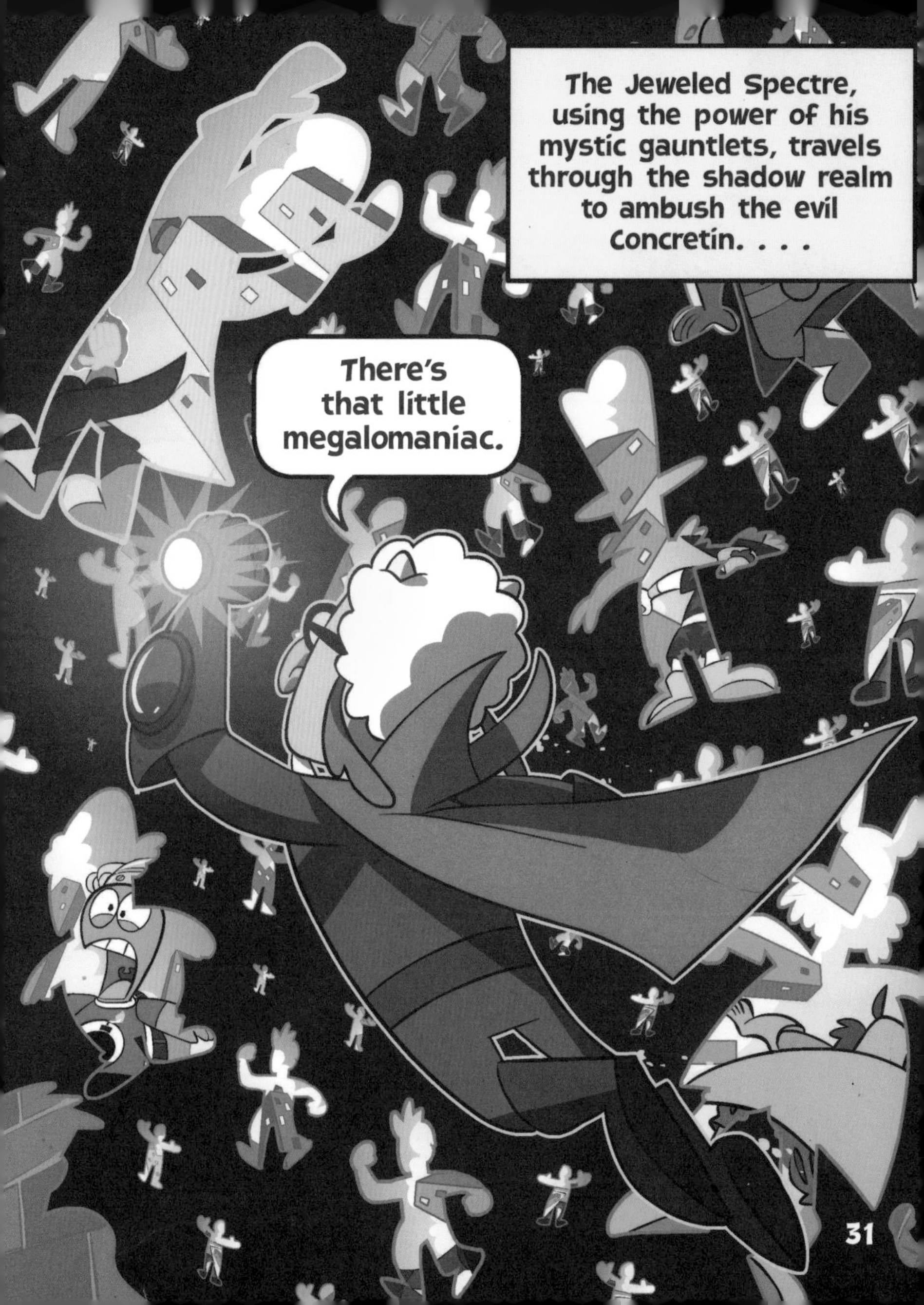
The Jeweled Spectre, using the power of his mystic gauntlets, travels through the shadow realm to ambush the evil Concretin. . . .
There's that little megalomaniac.

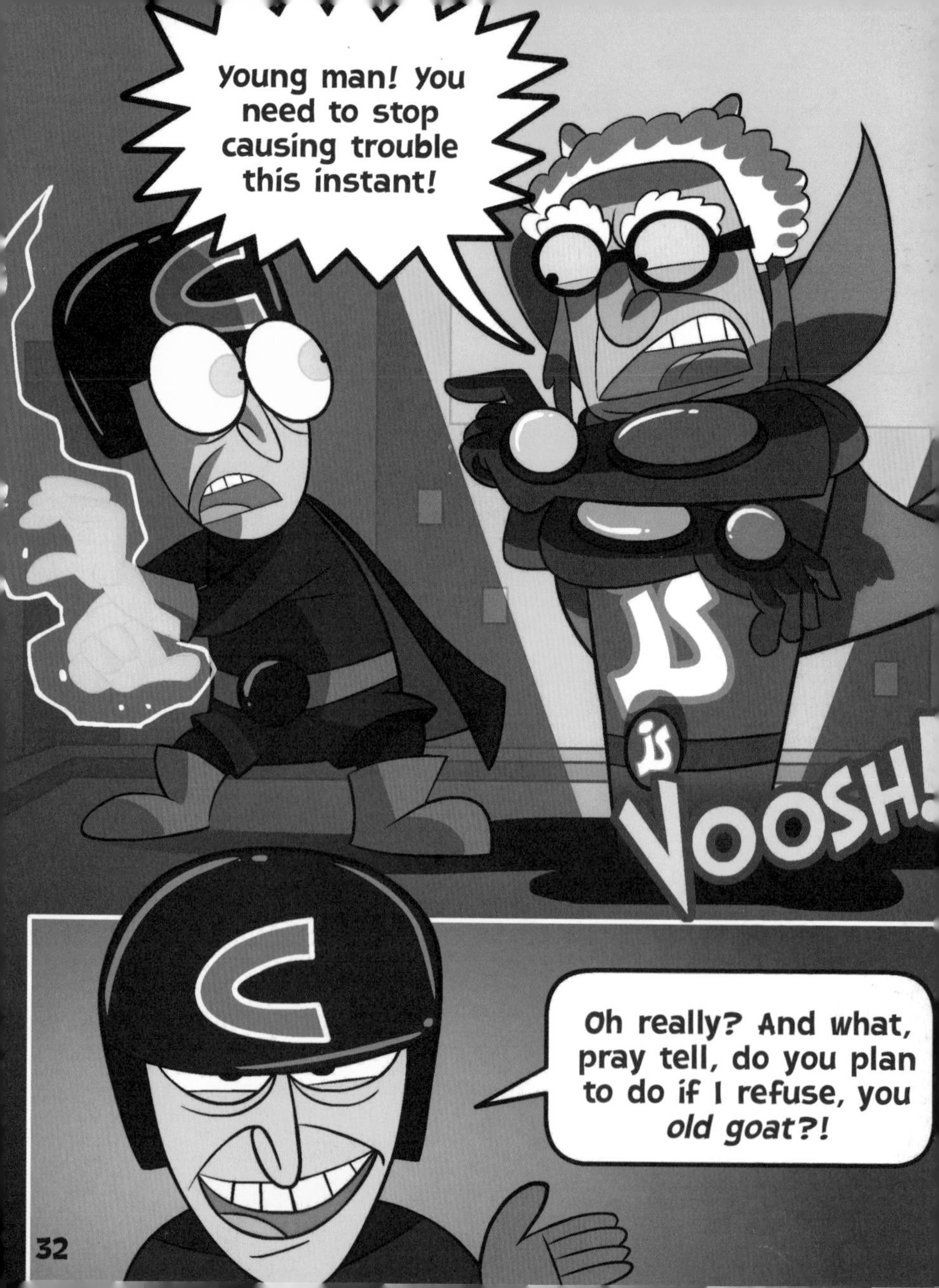
Young man! You need to stop causing trouble this instant!
VOOSH!
Oh really? And what, pray tell, do you plan to do if I refuse, you *old goat*?!

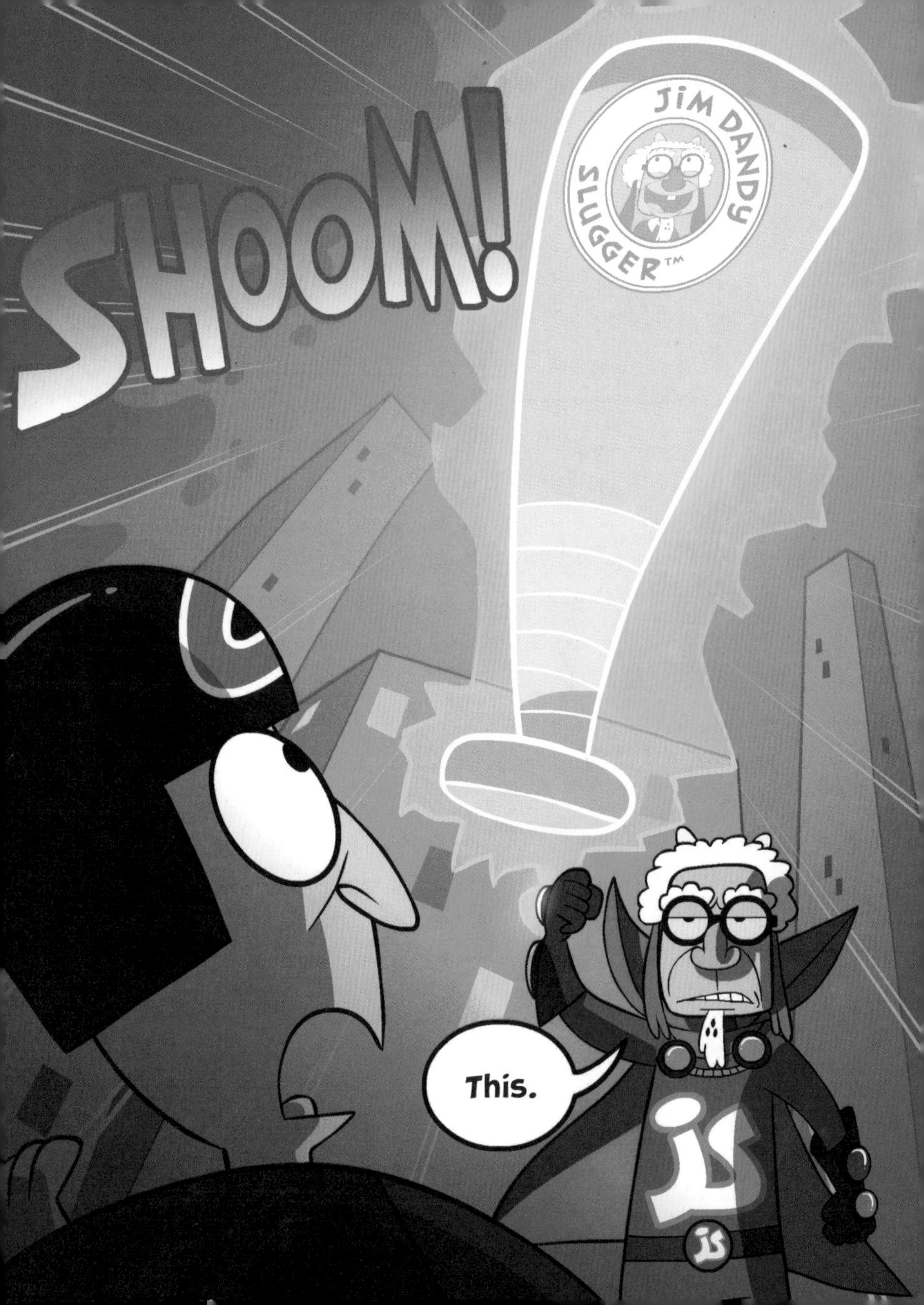
SHOOM!
JIM DANDY SLUGGER™
This.

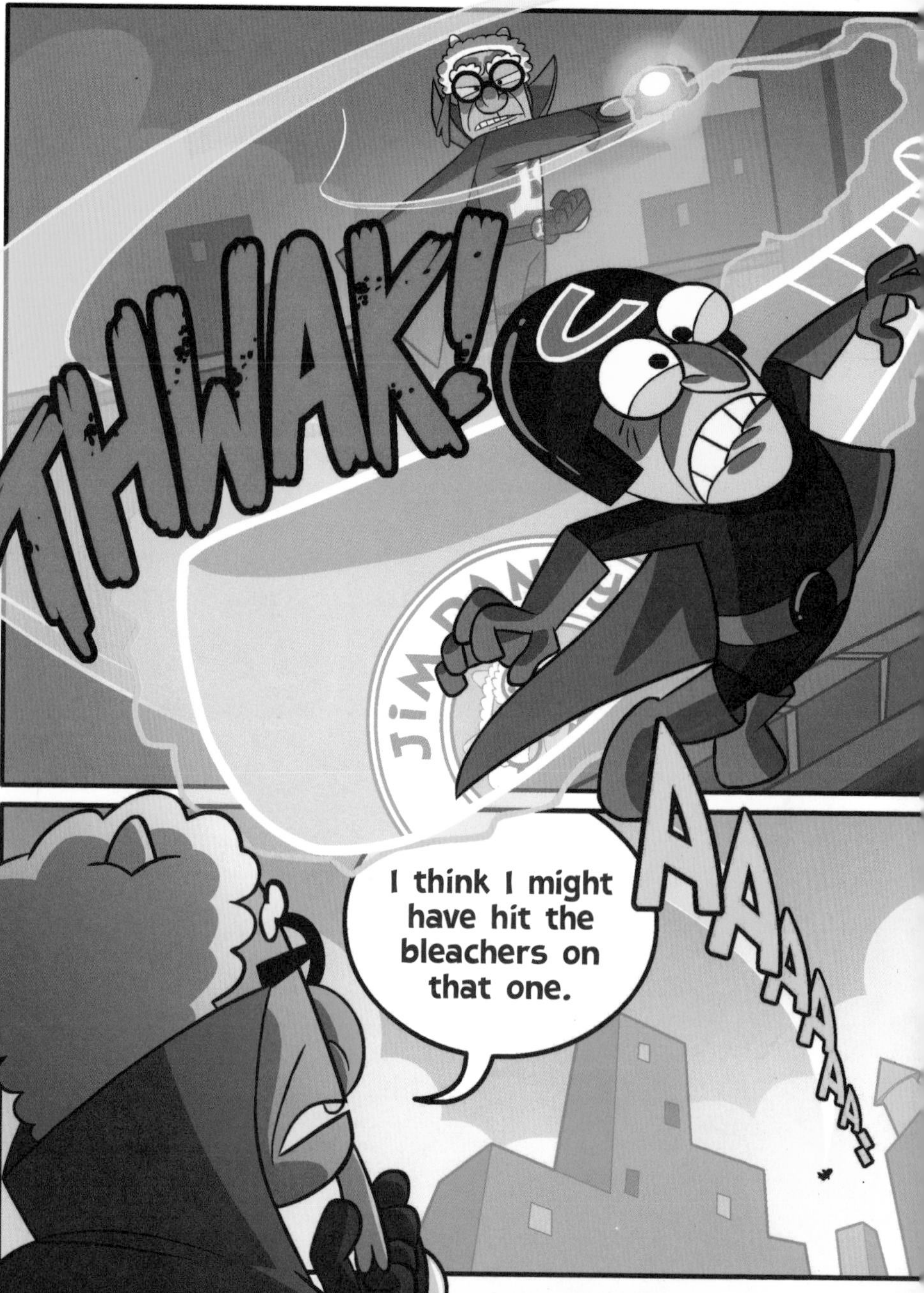
THWAK!
I think I might have hit the bleachers on that one.
AAAAAAA!

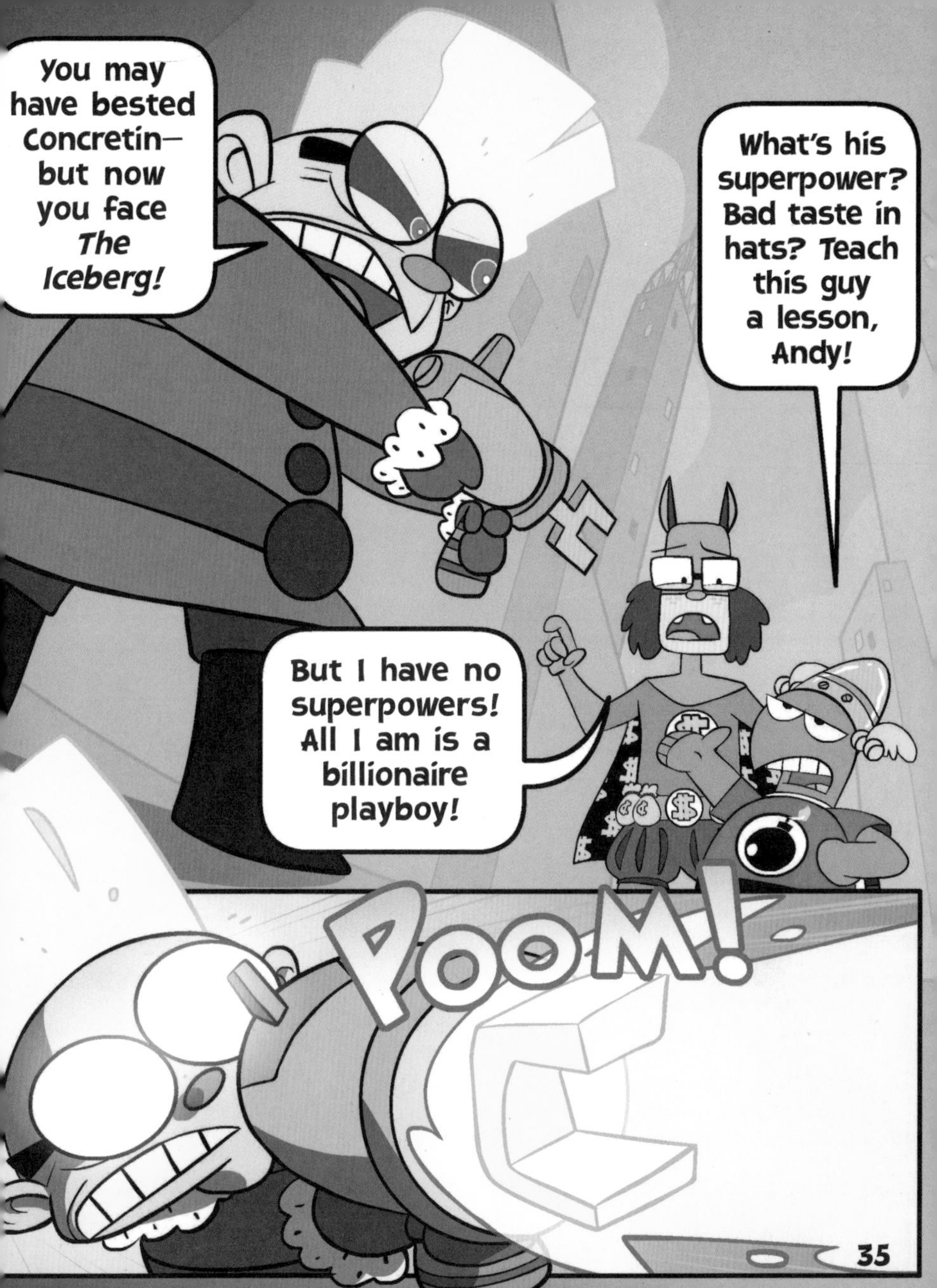
You may have bested Concretin— but now you face *The Iceberg!*
What's his superpower? Bad taste in hats? Teach this guy a lesson, Andy!
But I have no superpowers! All I am is a billionaire playboy!
POOM!

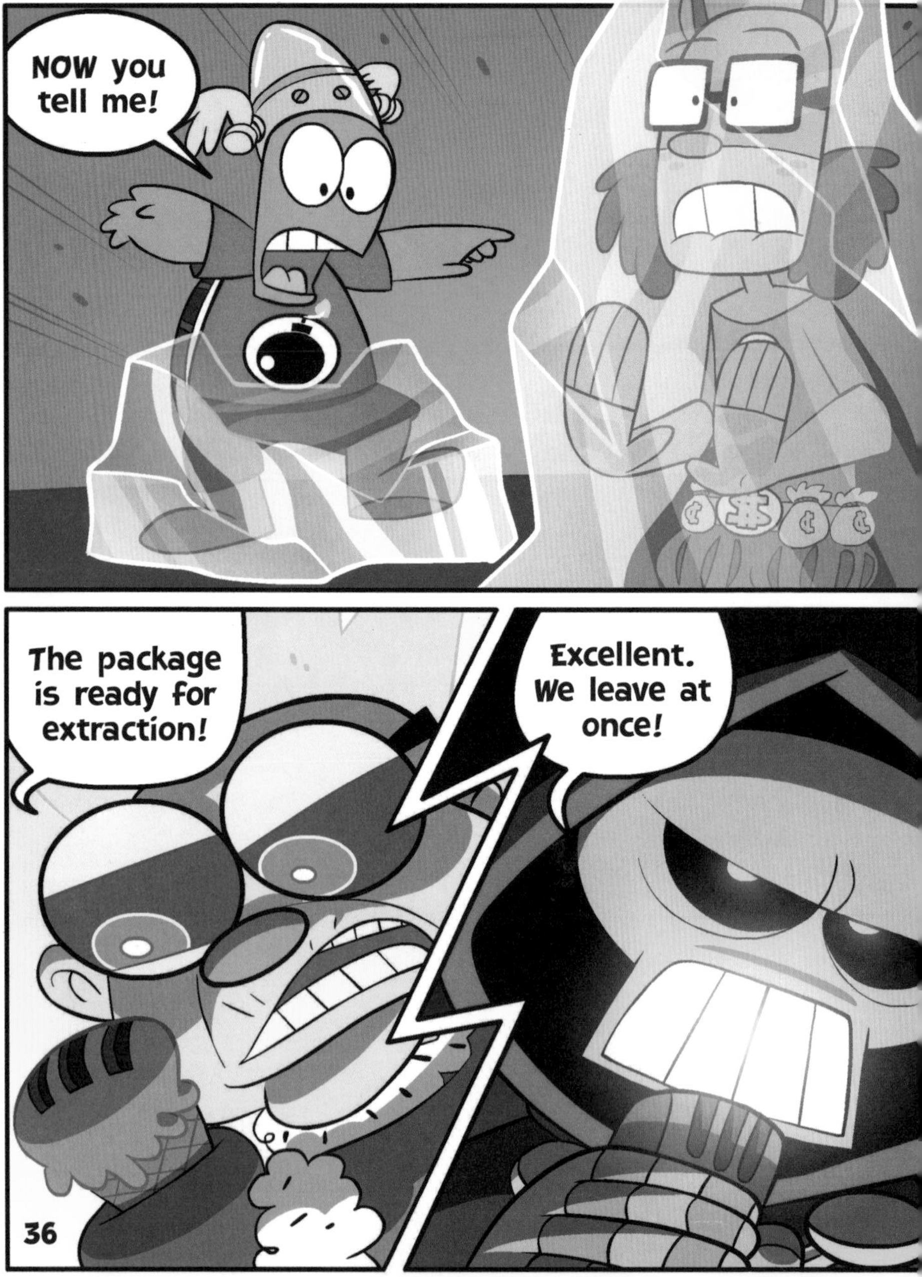
NOW you tell me!
The package is ready for extraction!
Excellent. We leave at once!

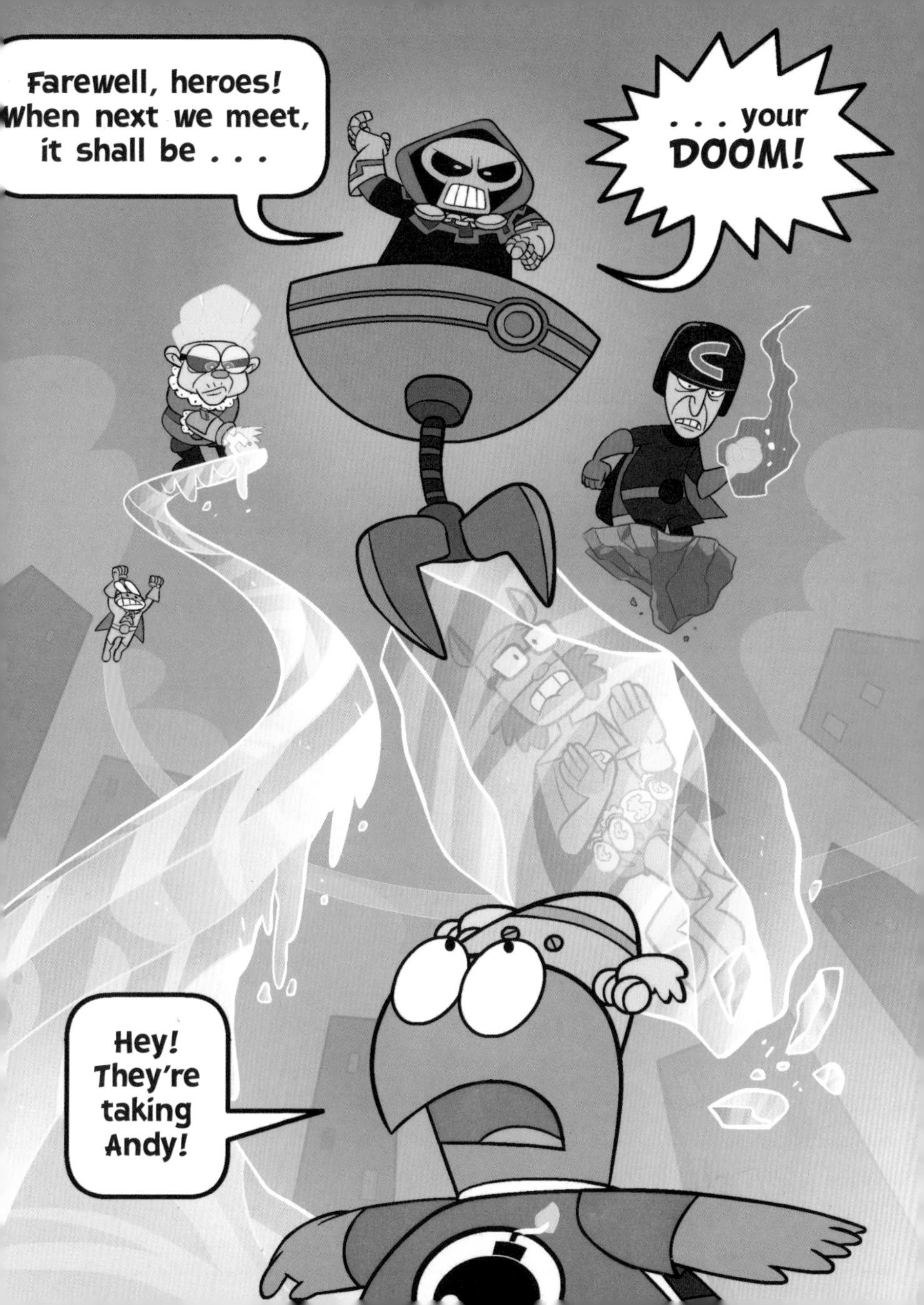
Farewell, heroes! When next we meet, it shall be . . .
. . . your DOOM!
Hey! They're taking Andy!

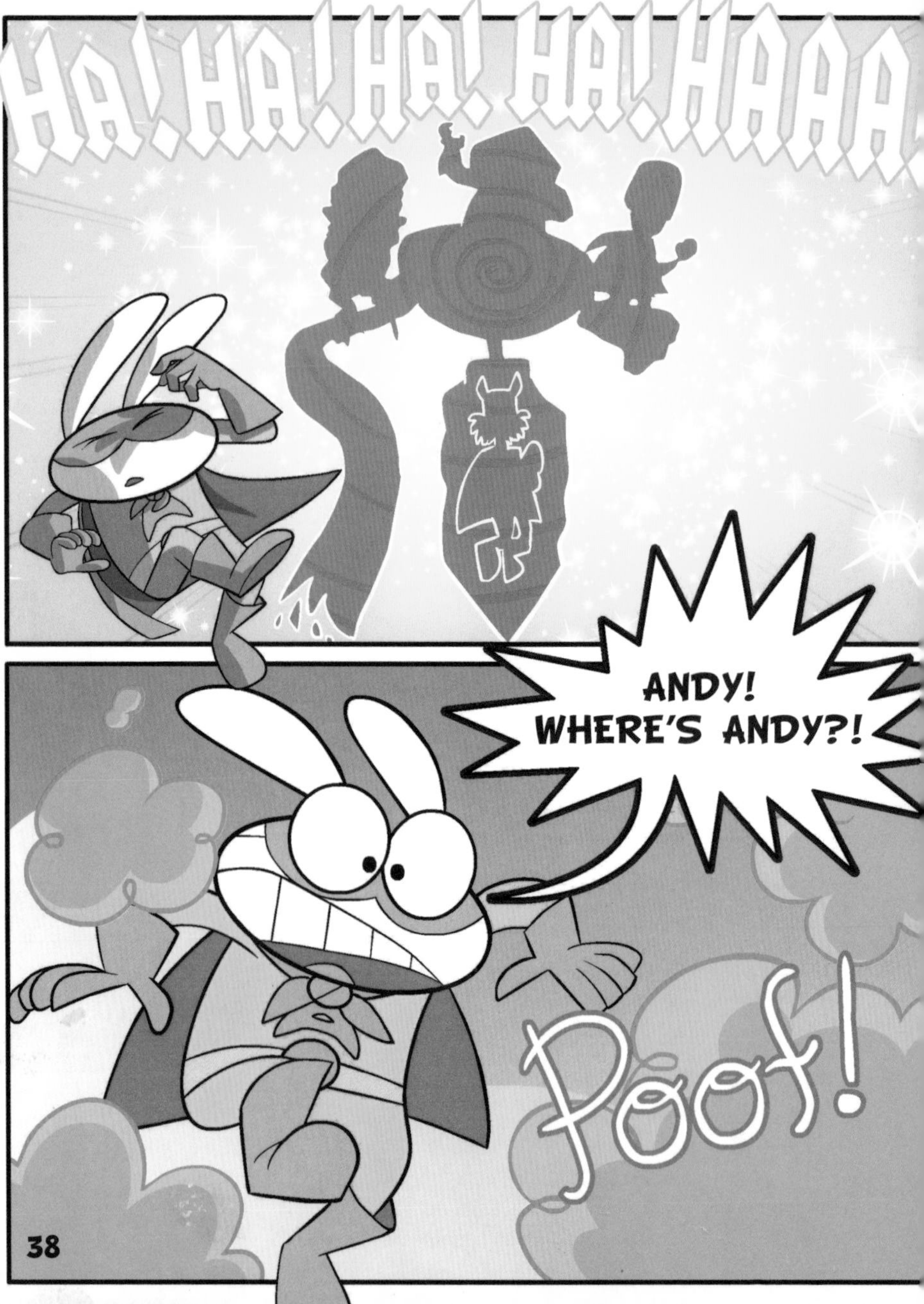
HA! HA! HA! HA! HAAAA
ANDY! WHERE'S ANDY?!
Poof!

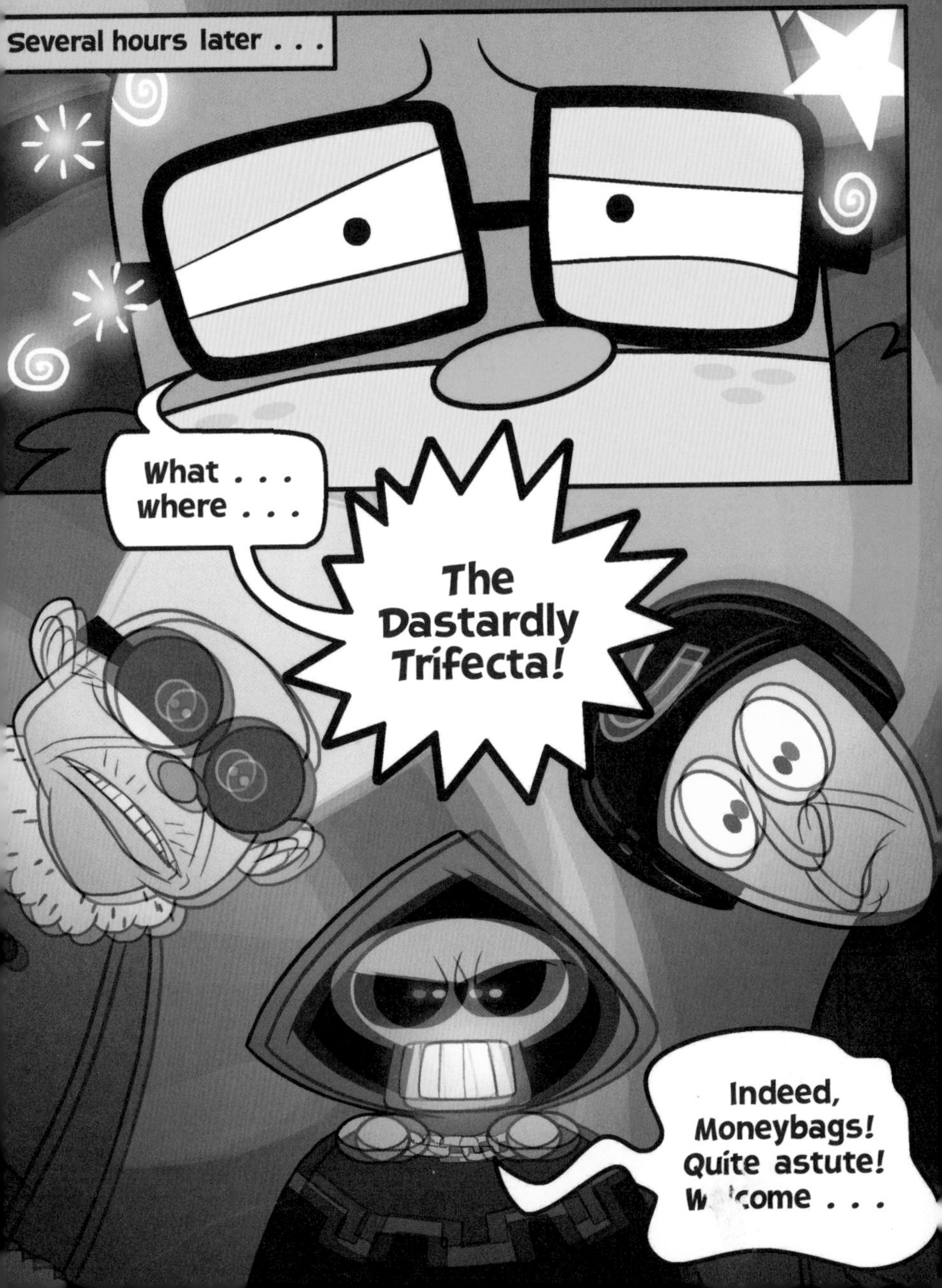
Several hours later . . .
What . . . where . . .
The Dastardly Trifecta!
Indeed, Moneybags! Quite astute! W come . . .

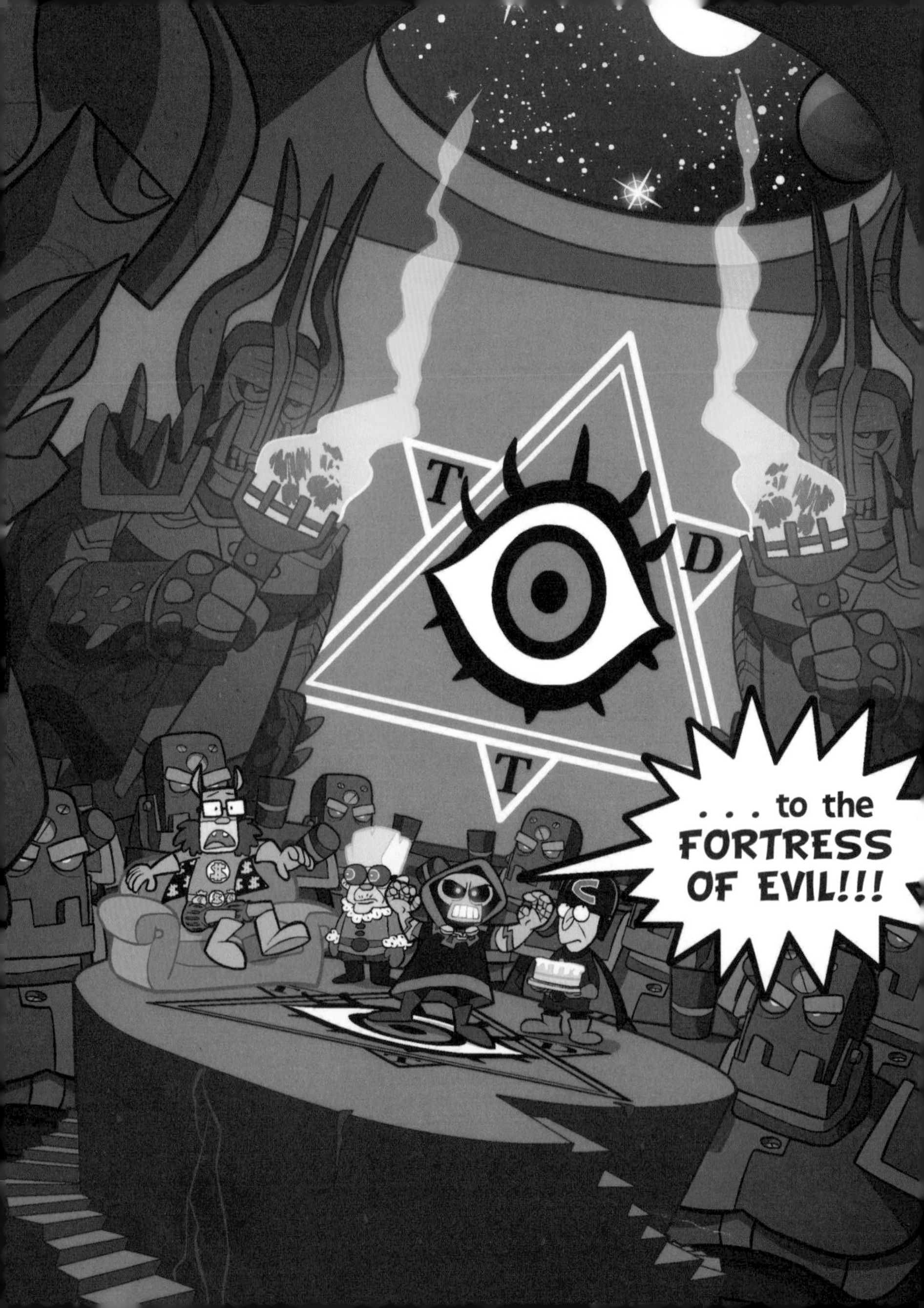
T
D
T
. . . to the FORTRESS OF EVIL!!!

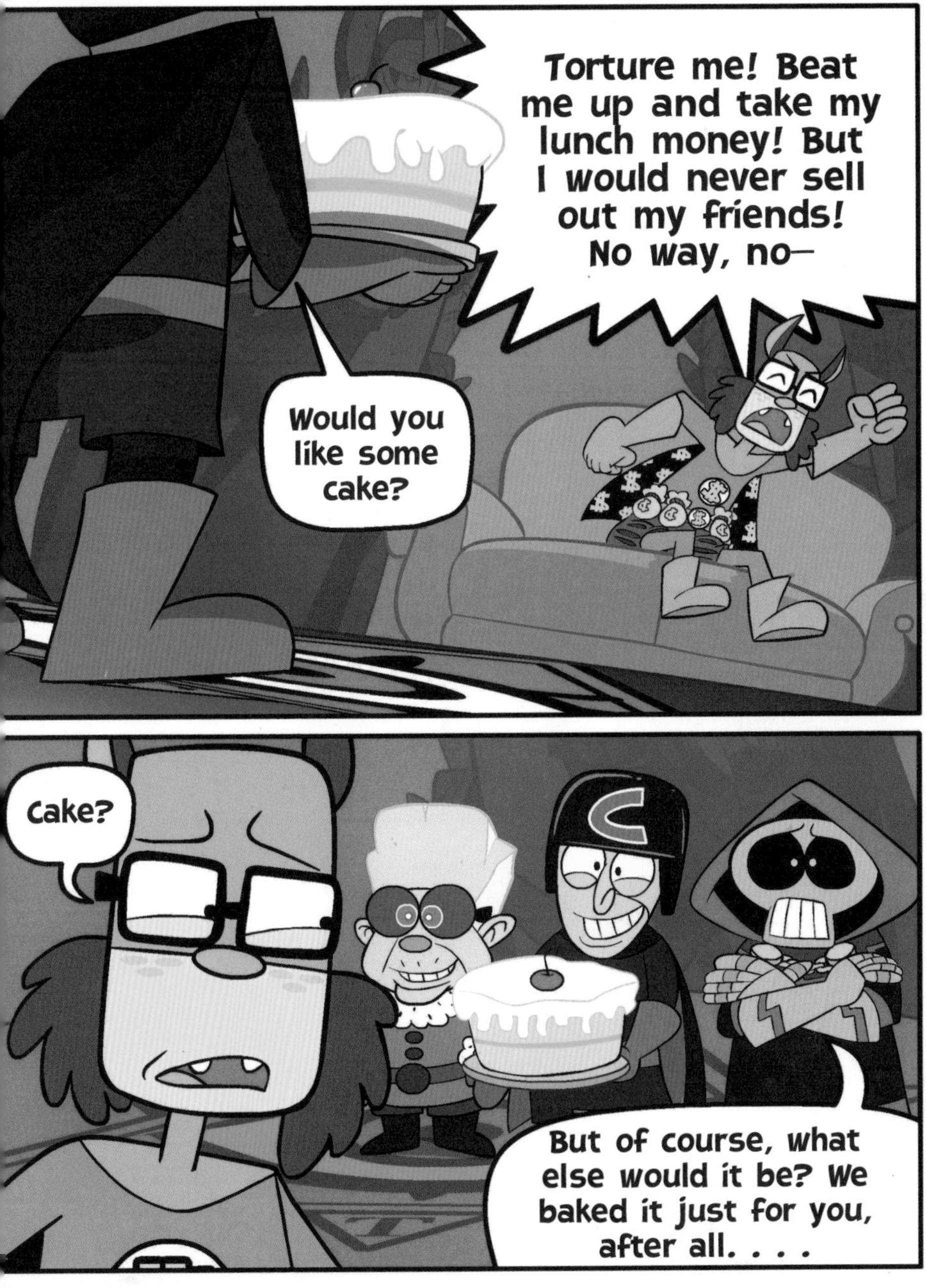
Torture me! Beat me up and take my lunch money! But I would never sell out my friends! No way, no—
Would you like some cake?
Cake?
But of course, what else would it be? We baked it just for you, after all. . . .

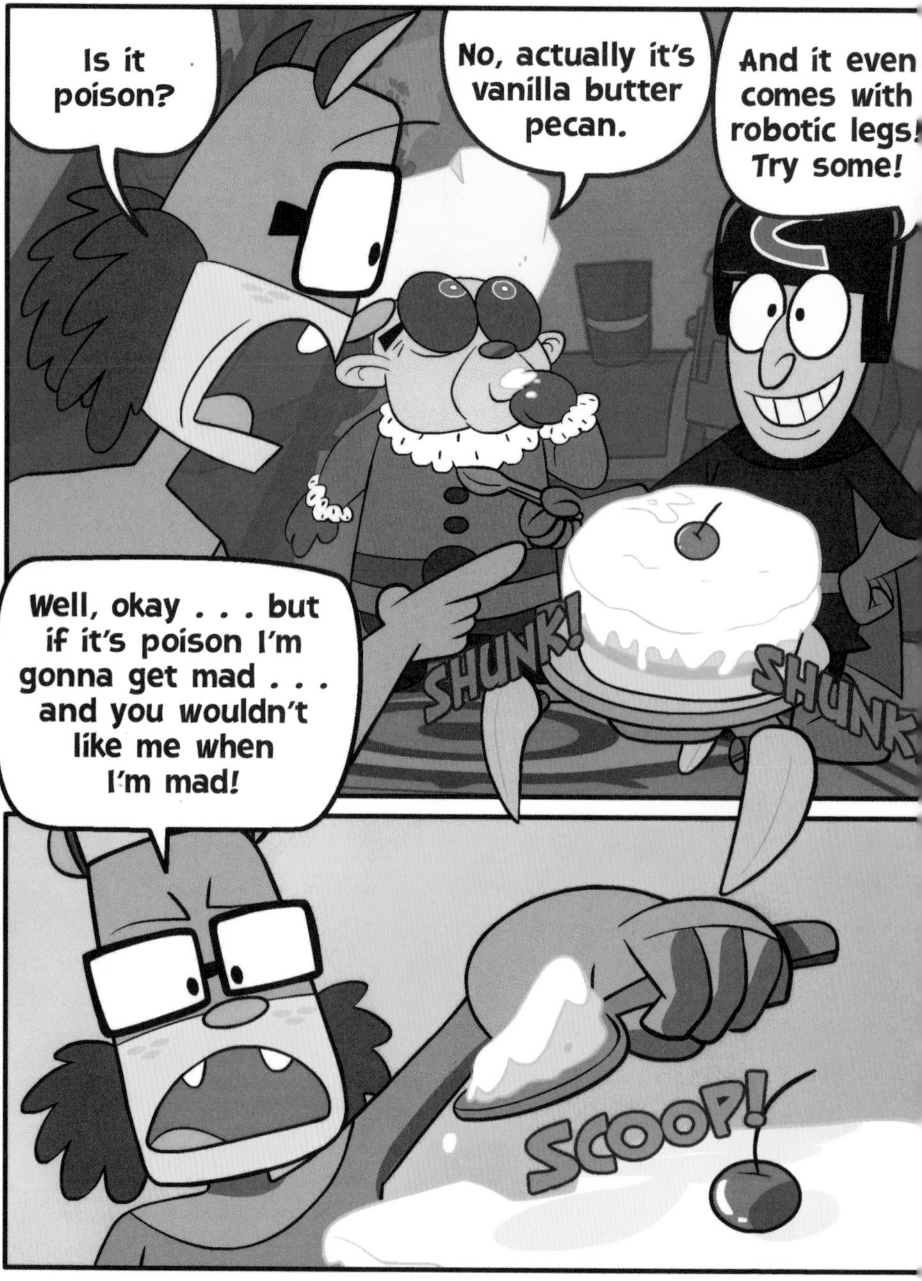

Is it poison?
No, actually it's vanilla butter pecan.
And it even comes with robotic legs! Try some!
SHUNK!
SHUNK
Well, okay . . . but if it's poison I'm gonna get mad . . . and you wouldn't like me when I'm mad!
SCOOP!

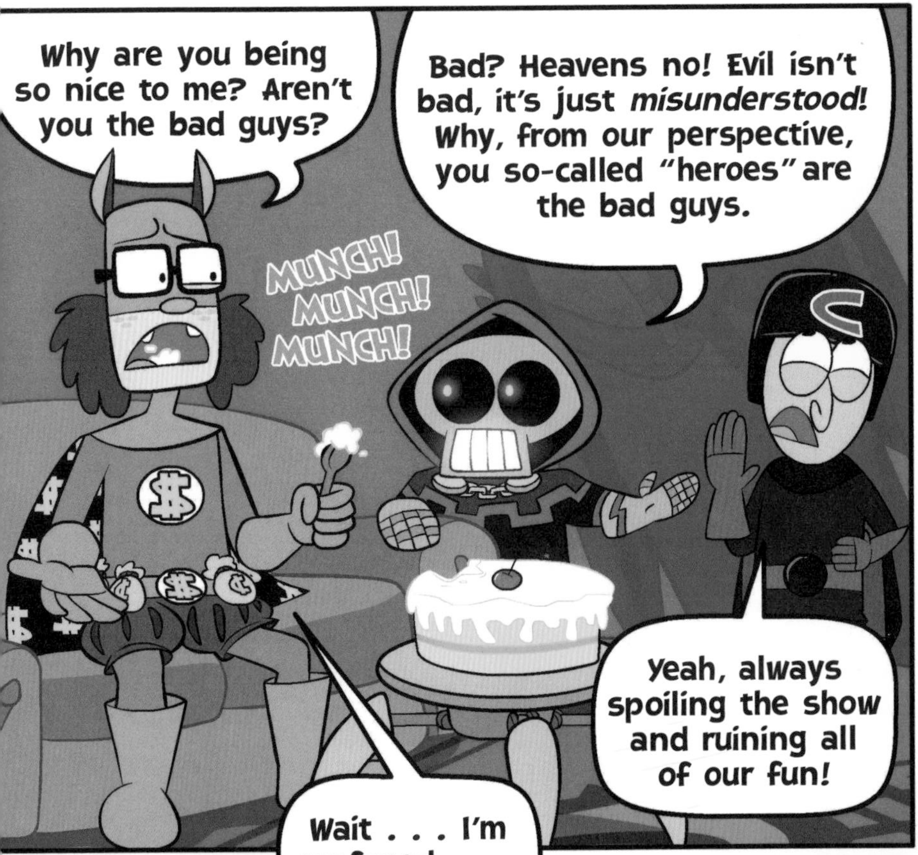
Why are you being so nice to me? Aren't you the bad guys?
Bad? Heavens no! Evil isn't bad, it's just *misunderstood*! Why, from our perspective, you so-called "heroes" are the bad guys.
MUNCH! MUNCH! MUNCH!
Yeah, always spoiling the show and ruining all of our fun!
Wait . . . I'm confused. . . .

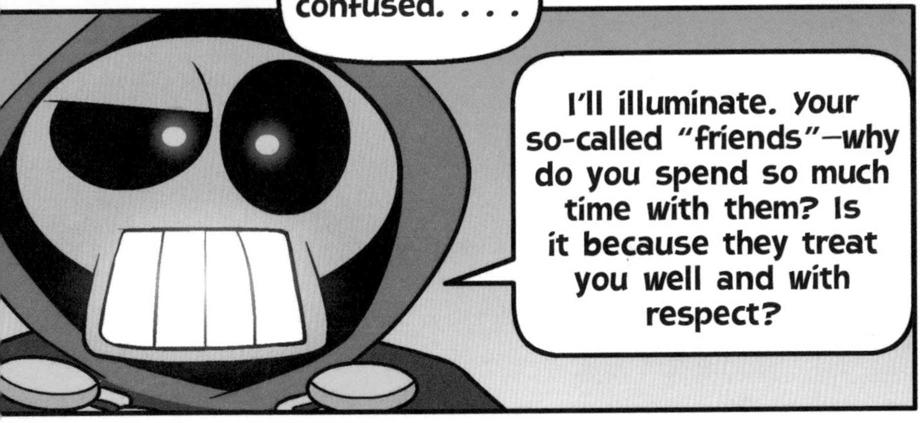
I'll illuminate. Your so-called "friends"—why do you spend so much time with them? Is it because they treat you well and with respect?

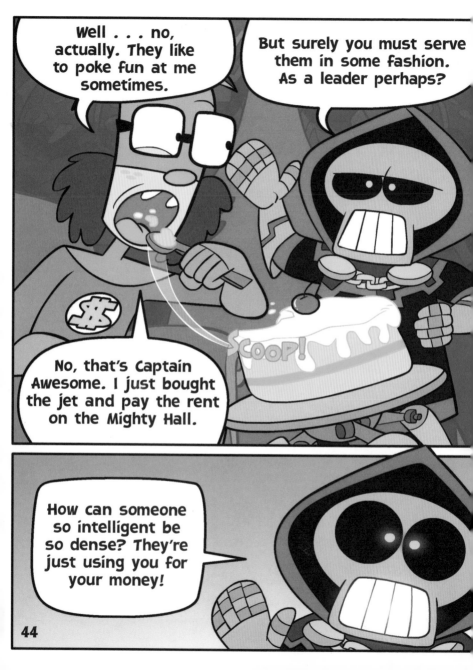

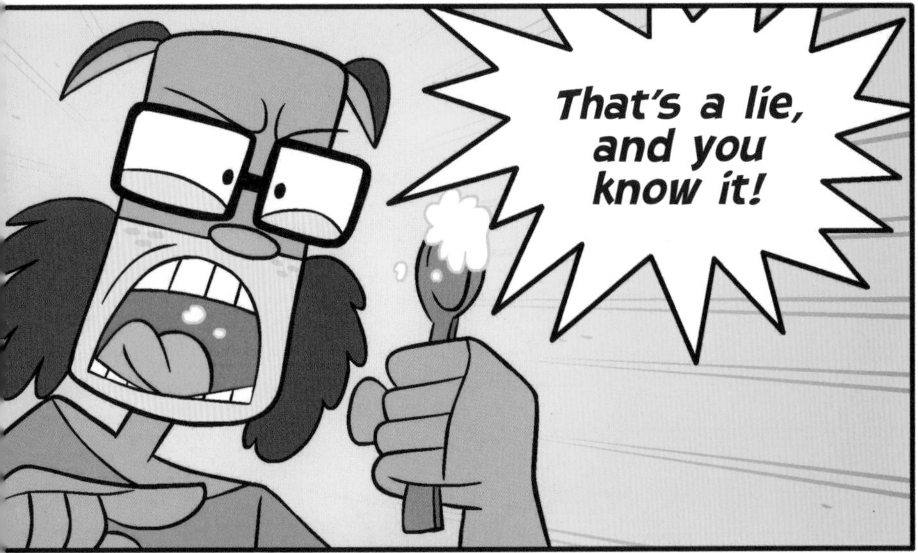
That's a lie, and you know it!

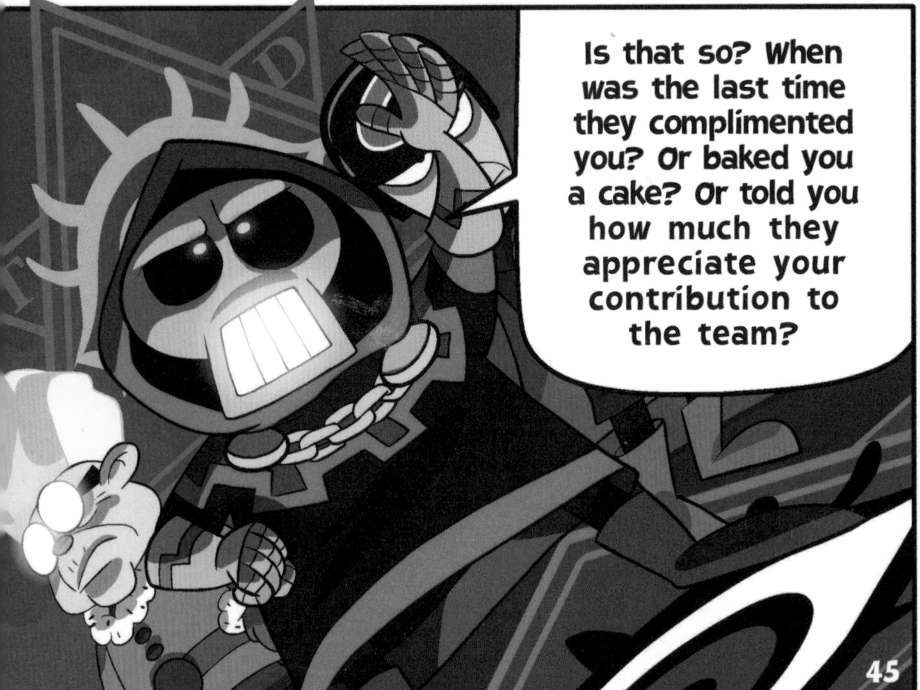
Is that so? When was the last time they complimented you? Or baked you a cake? Or told you how much they appreciate your contribution to the team?

47

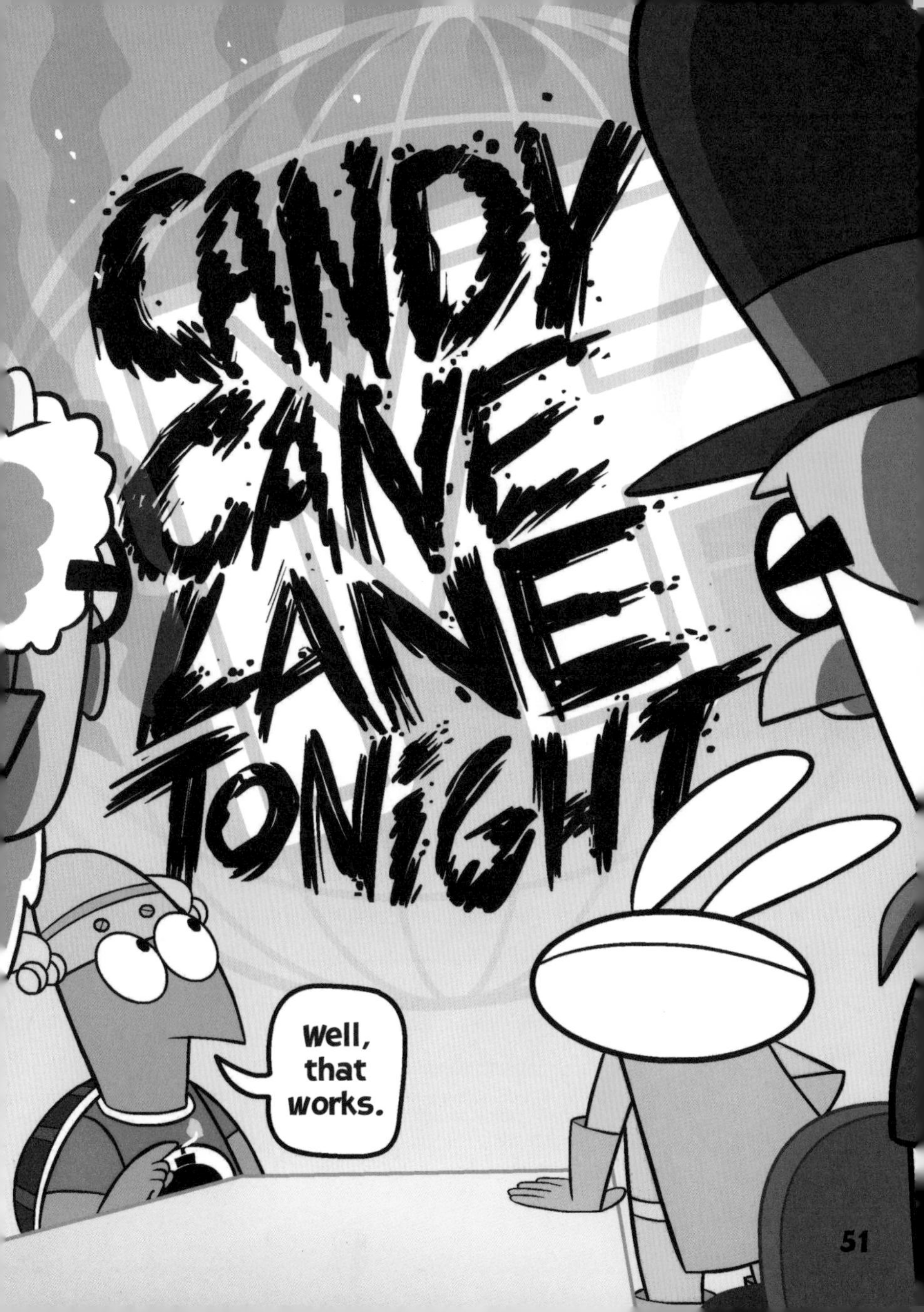
CANDY CANE LANE TONIGHT
Well, that works.

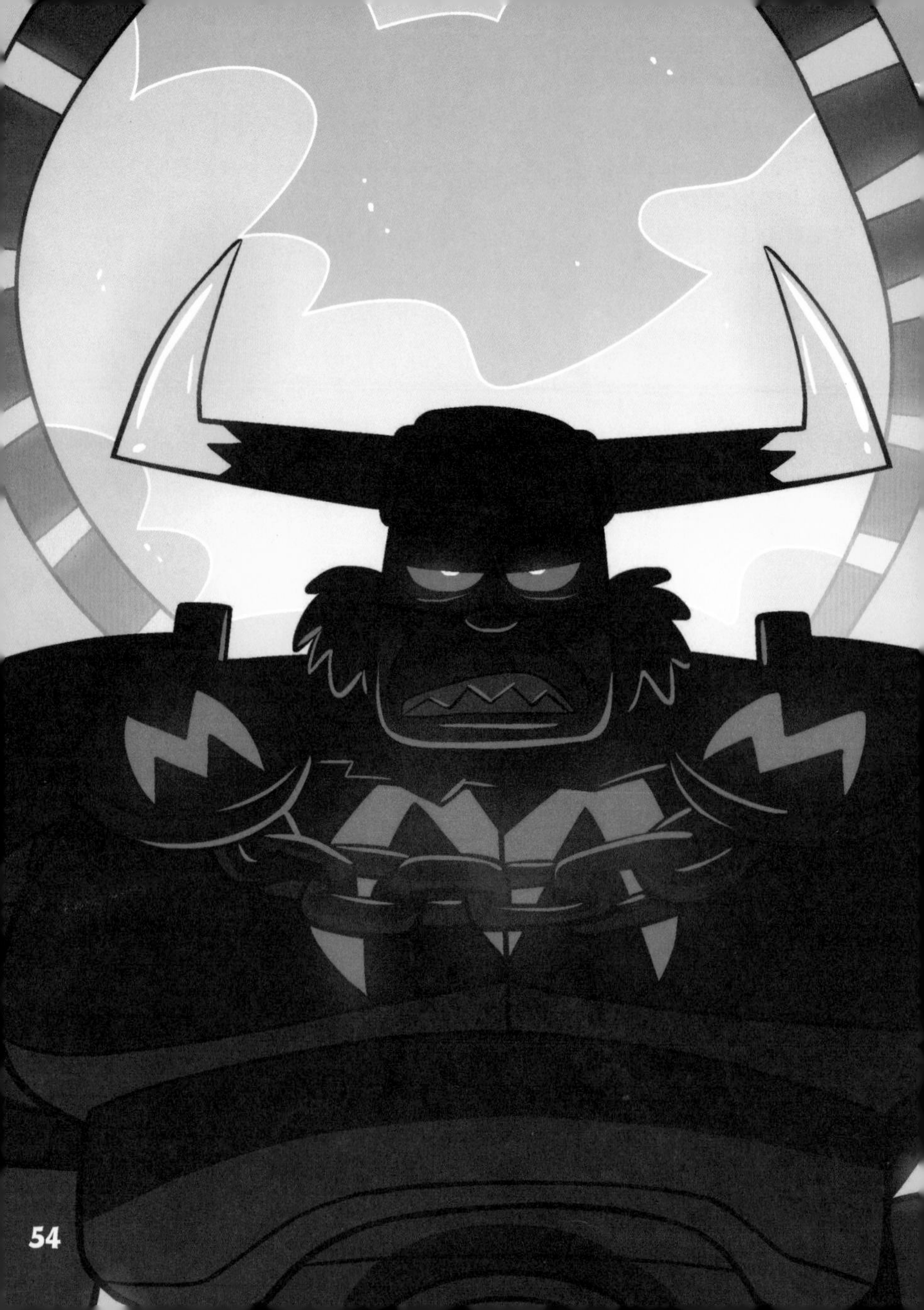

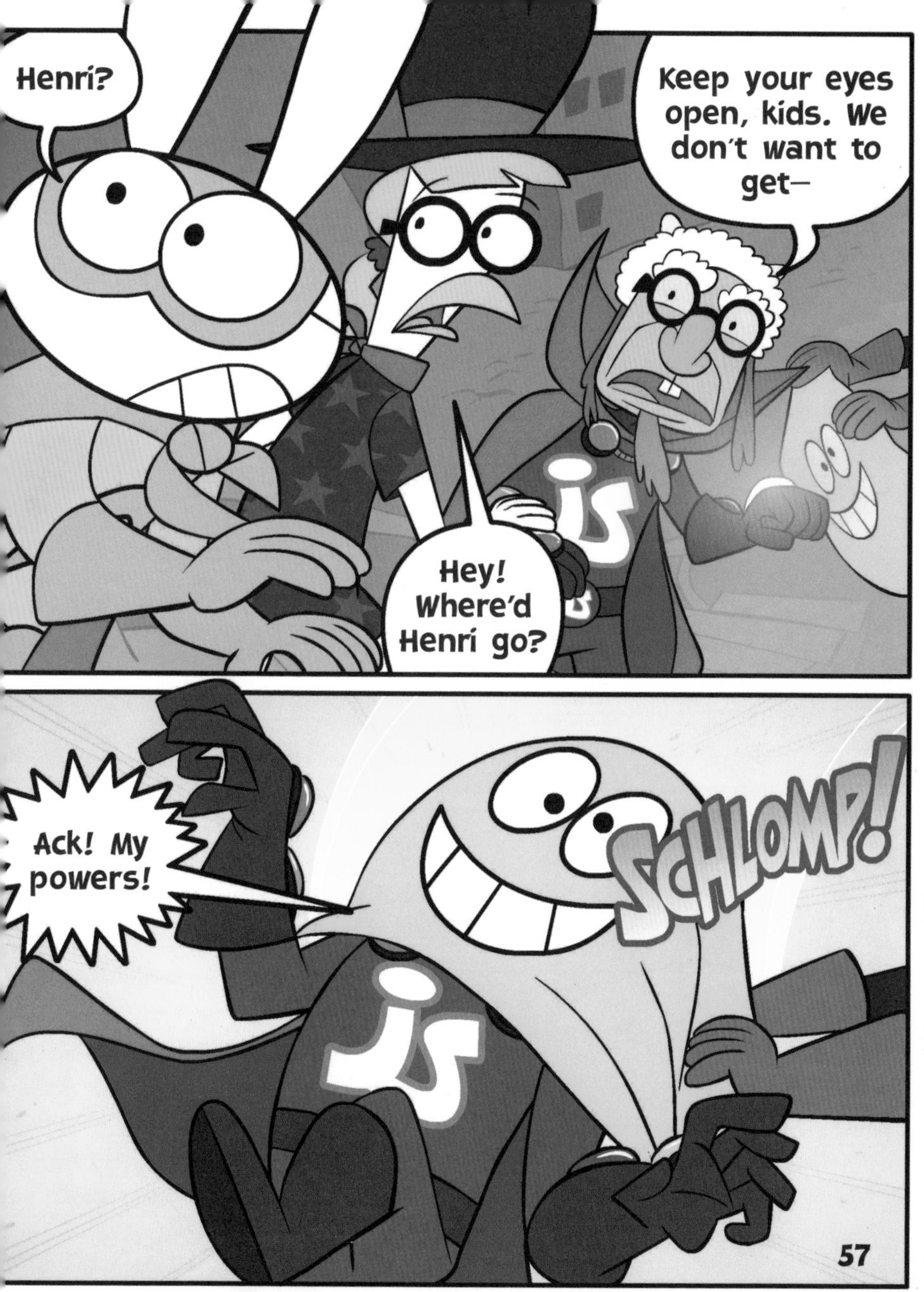
Henri?
Keep your eyes open, kids. We don't want to get–
Hey! Where'd Henri go?
Ack! My powers!
SCHLOMP!
JS
JS

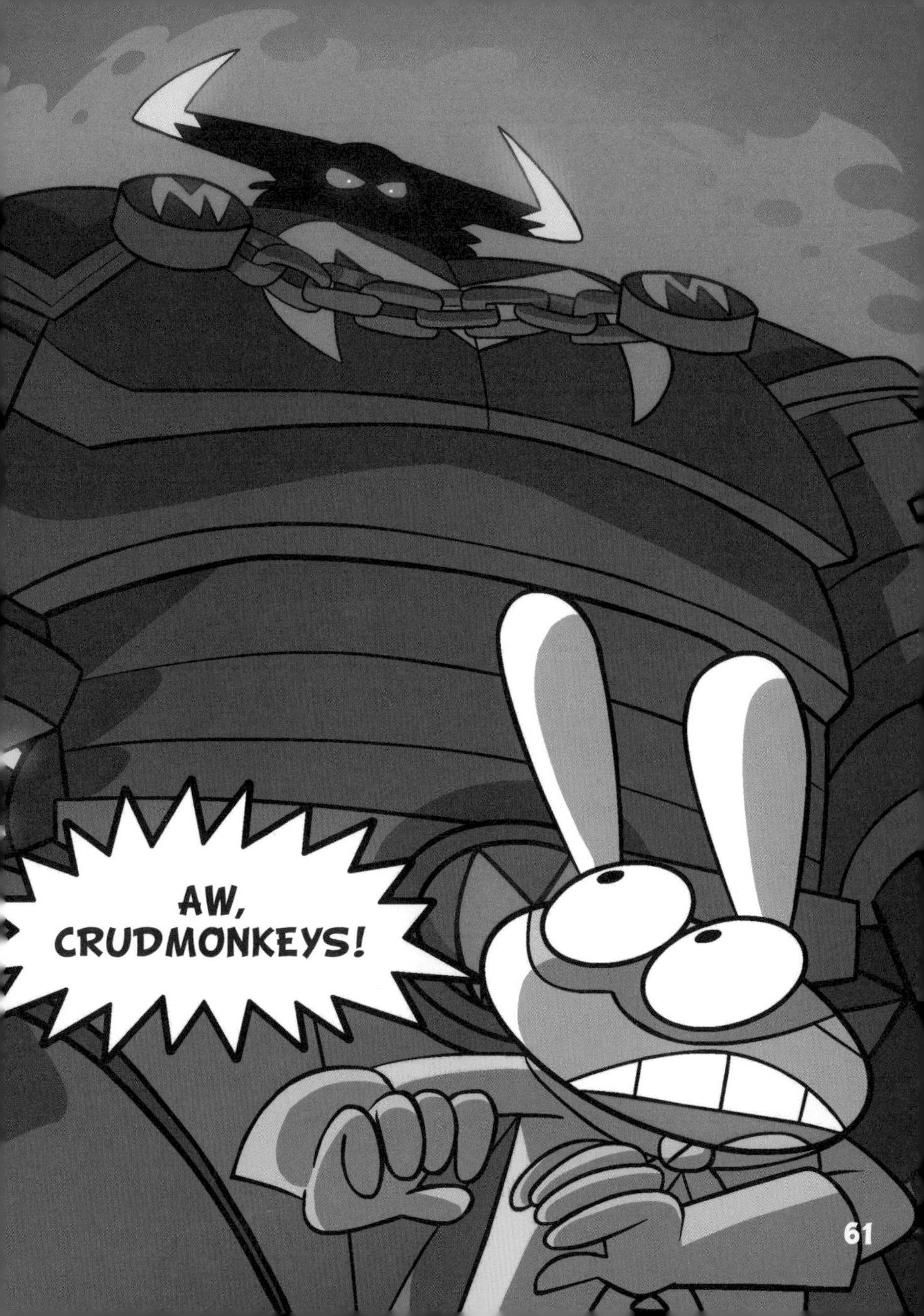
AW,
CRUDMONKEYS!

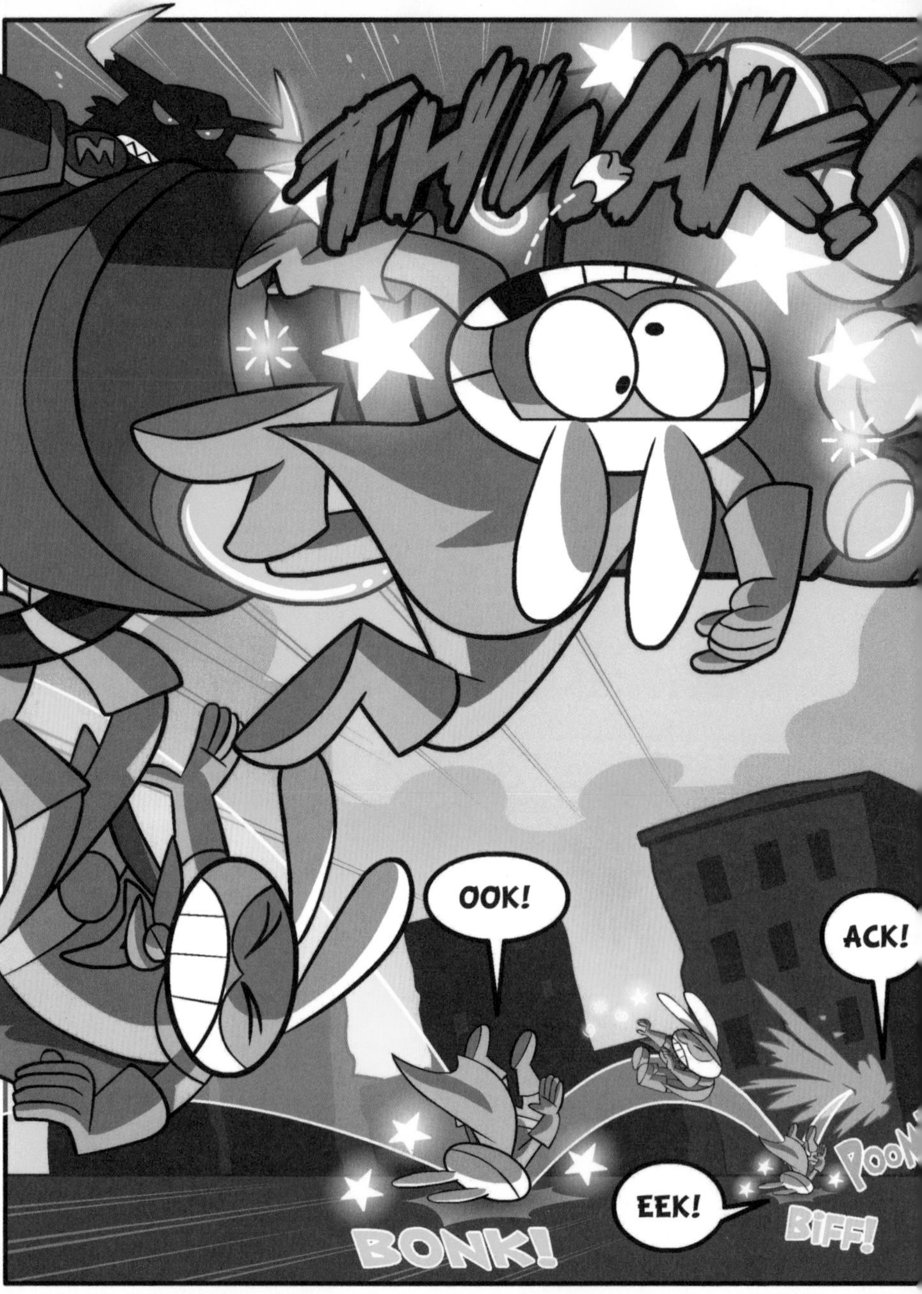
THWAK!
OOK!
ACK!
EEK!
BONK!
BIFF!

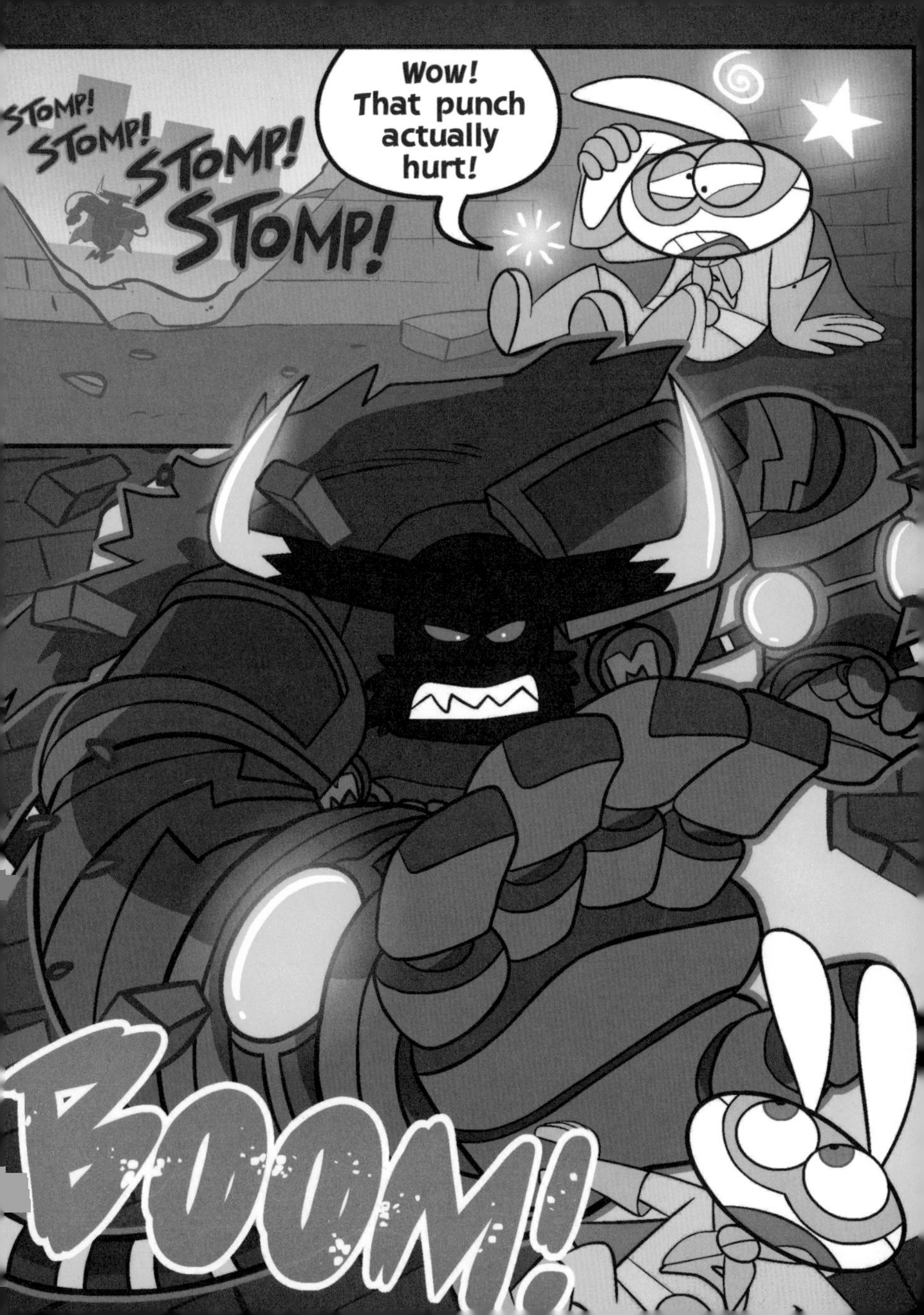
STOMP! STOMP! STOMP! STOMP!
Wow! That punch actually hurt!
BOOM!

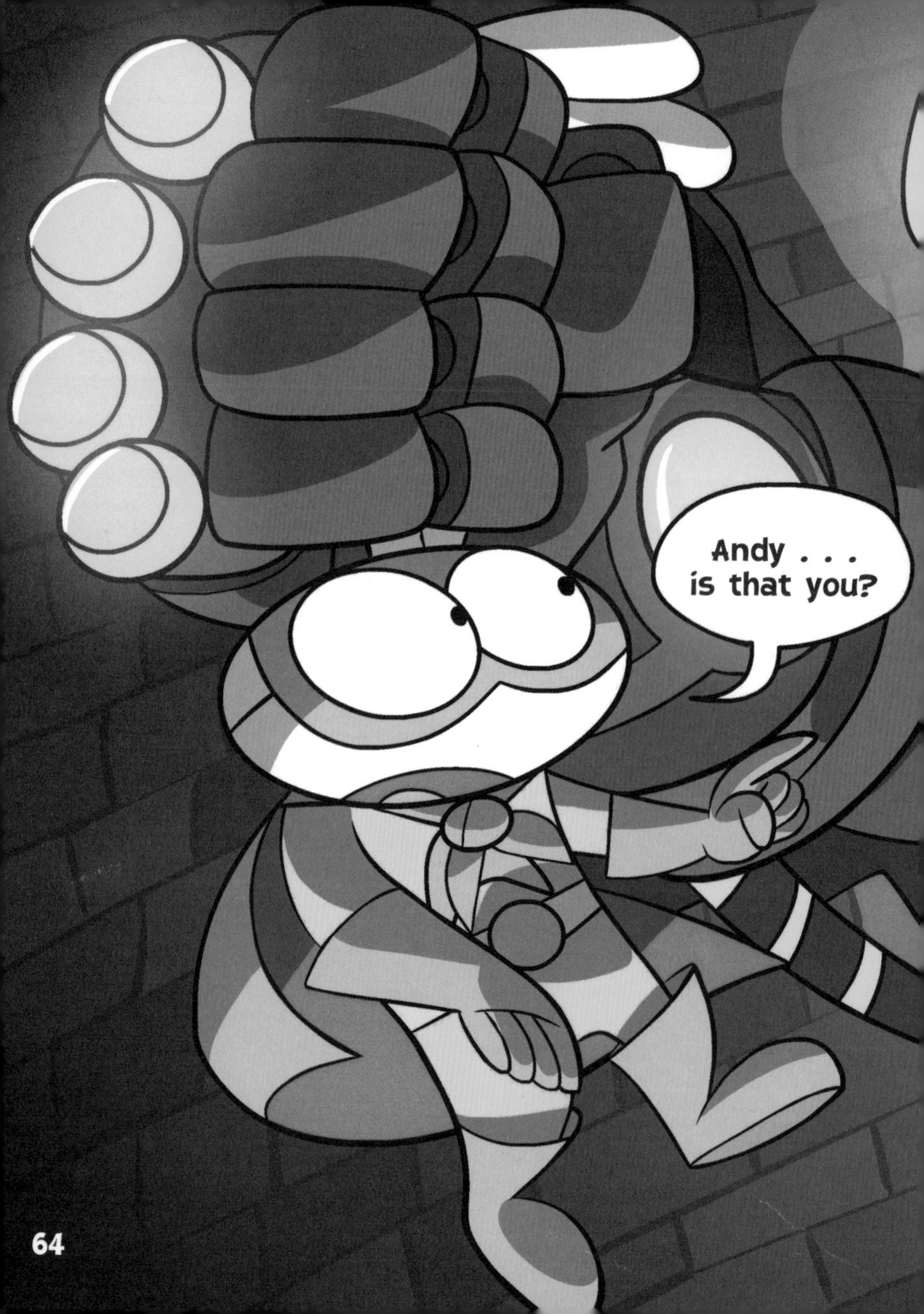
Andy . . . is that you?

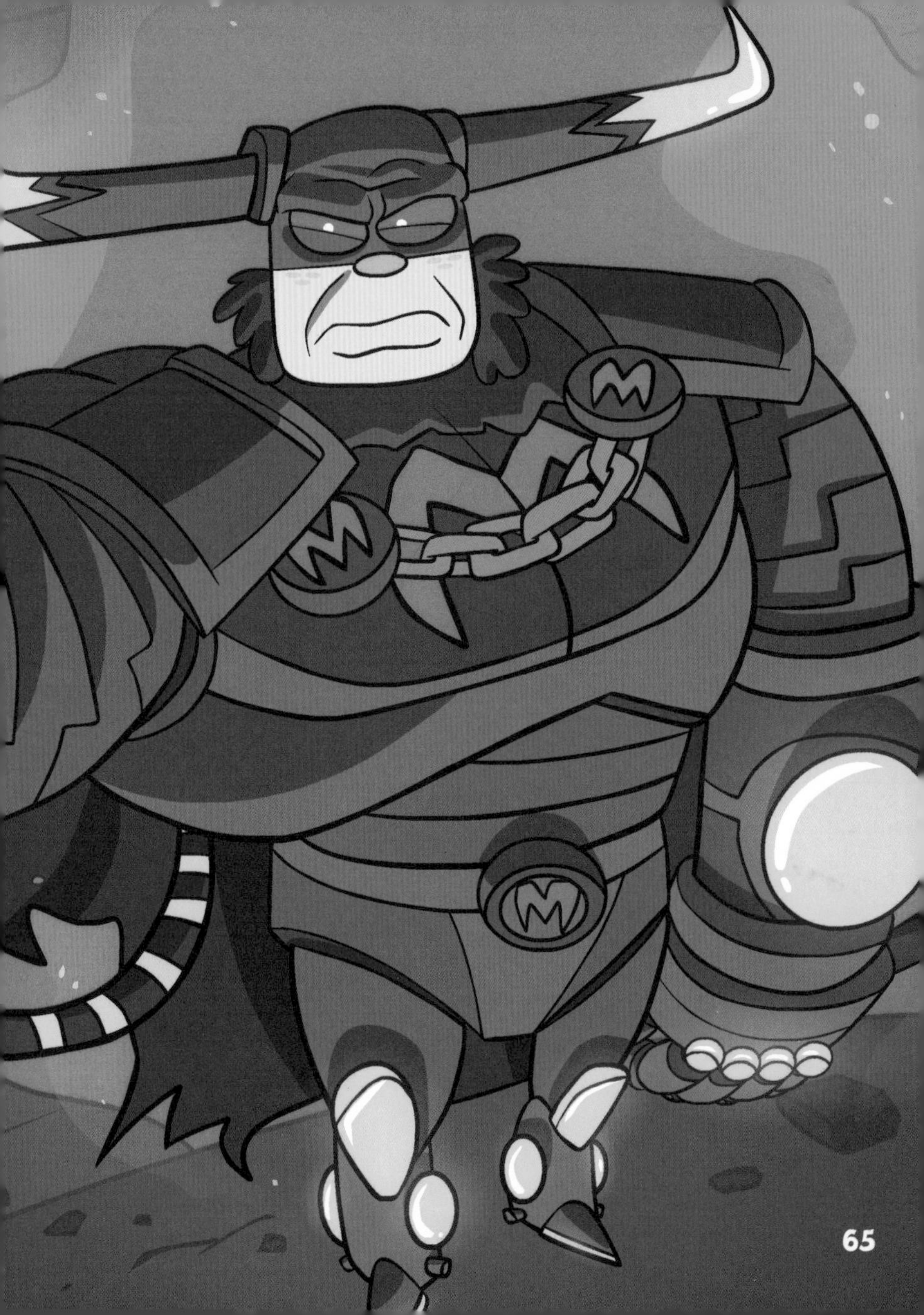

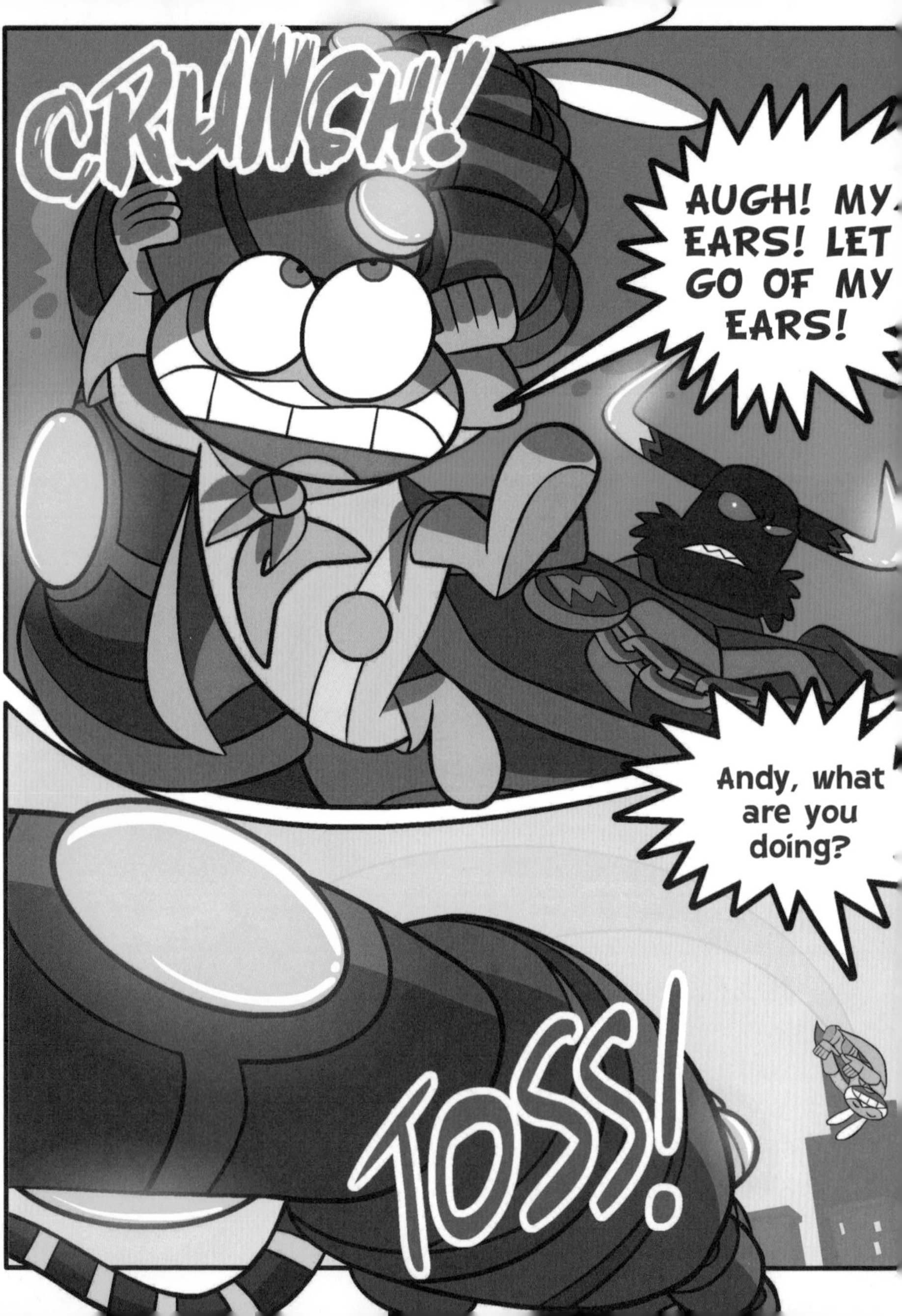
CRUNCH!
AUGH! MY EARS! LET GO OF MY EARS!
Andy, what are you doing?
TOSS!

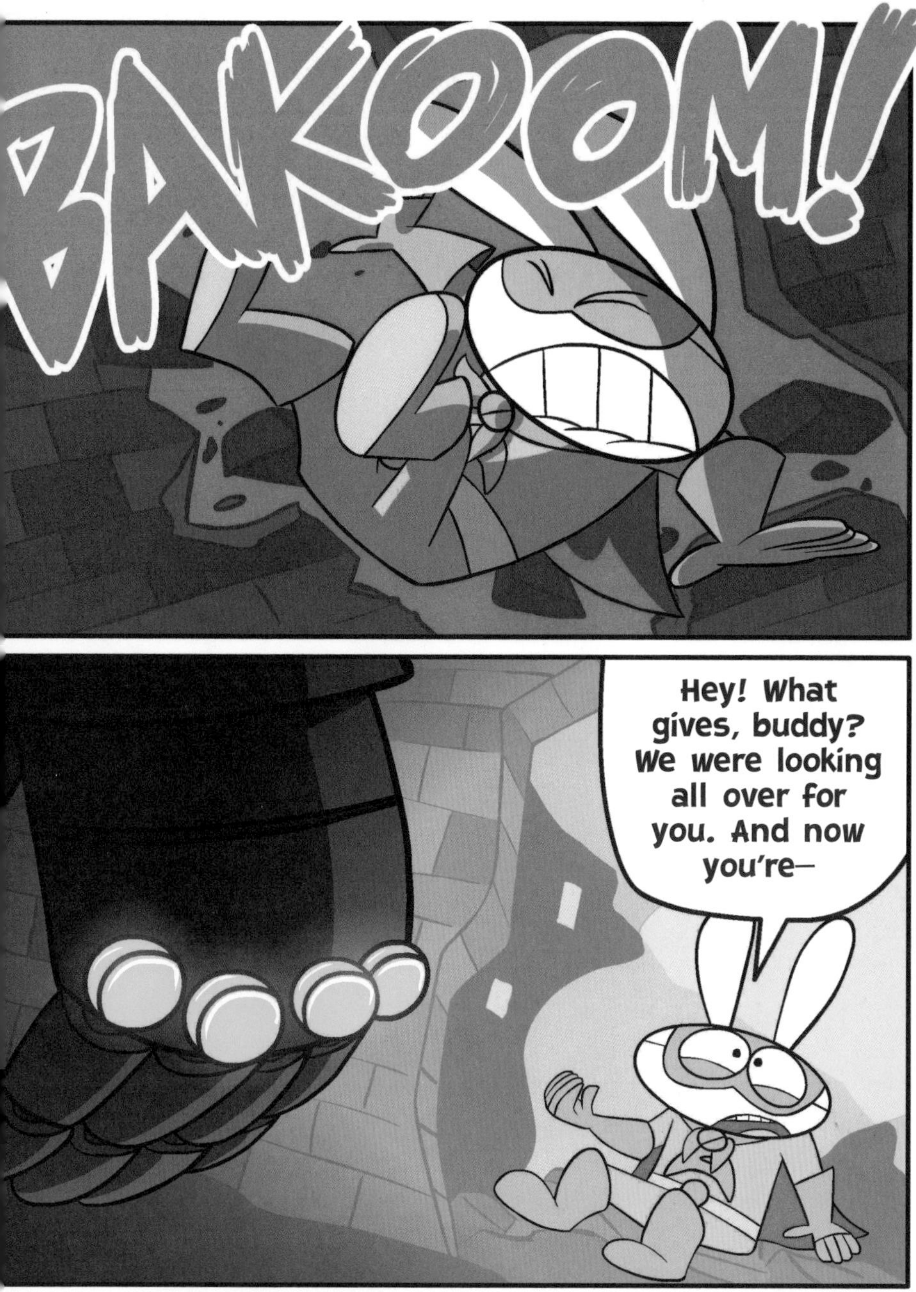
BAKOOM!
Hey! What gives, buddy? We were looking all over for you. And now you're—

68

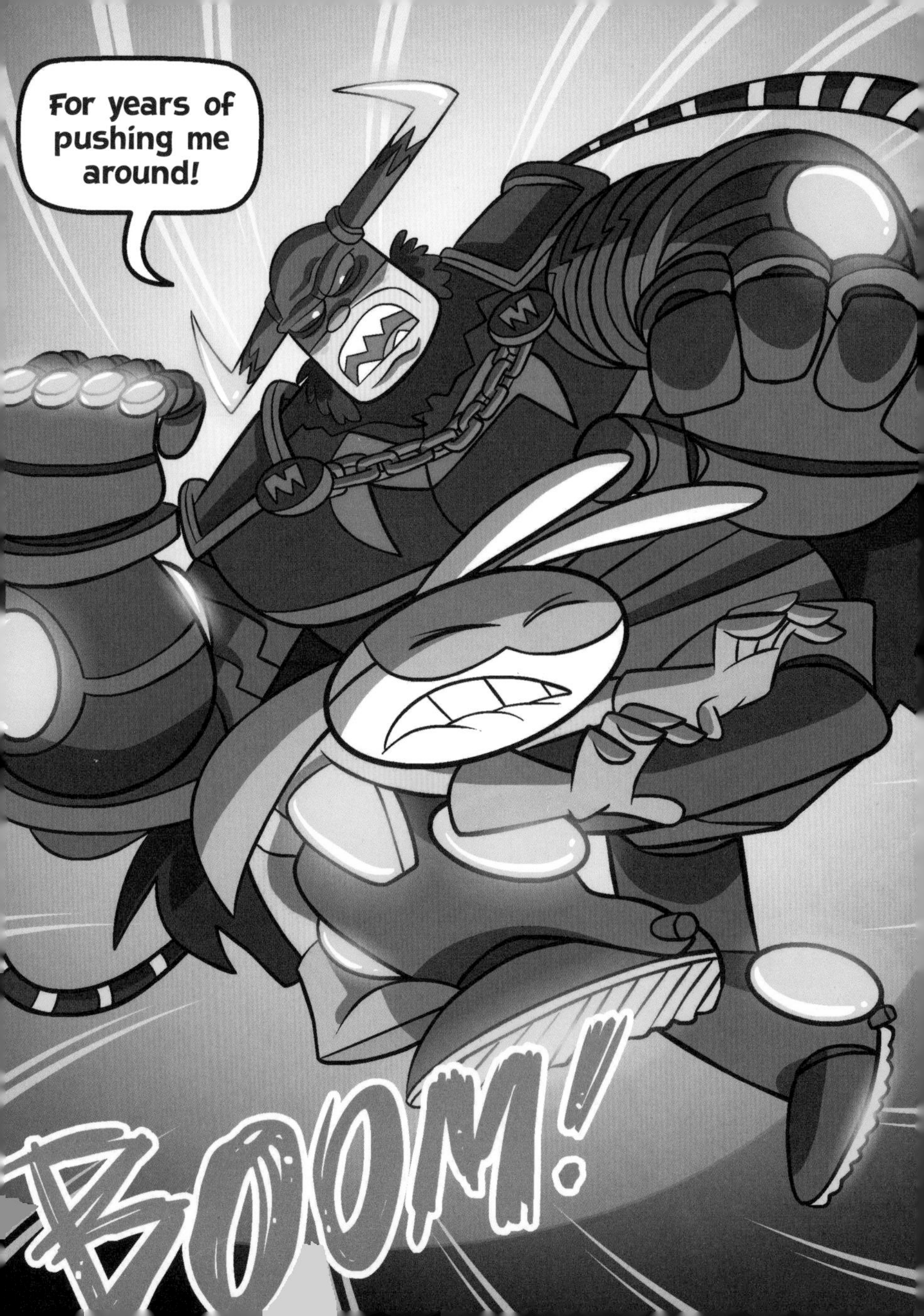
For years of pushing me around!
BOOM!

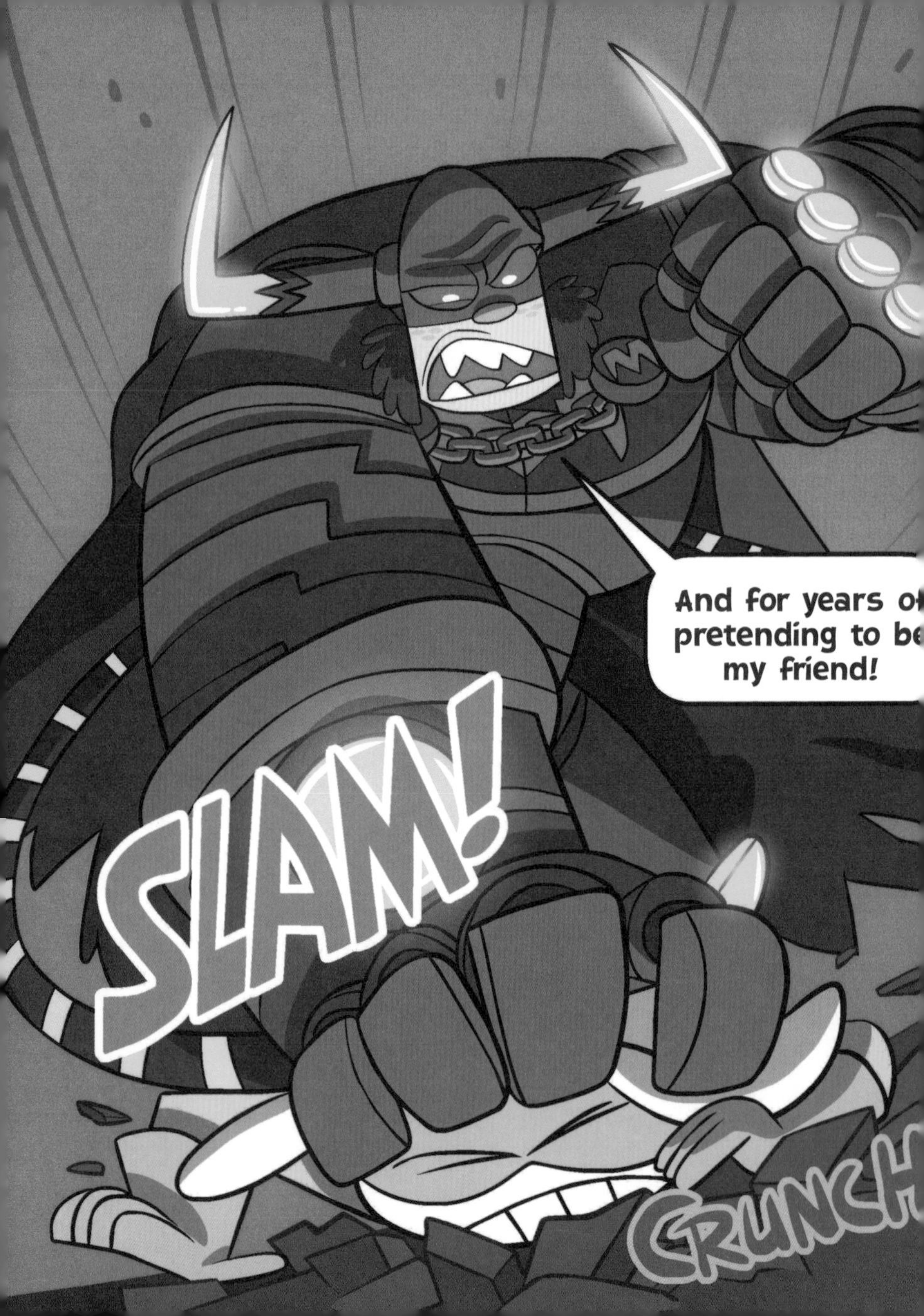
And for years o
pretending to be
my friend!
SLAM!
CRUNCH

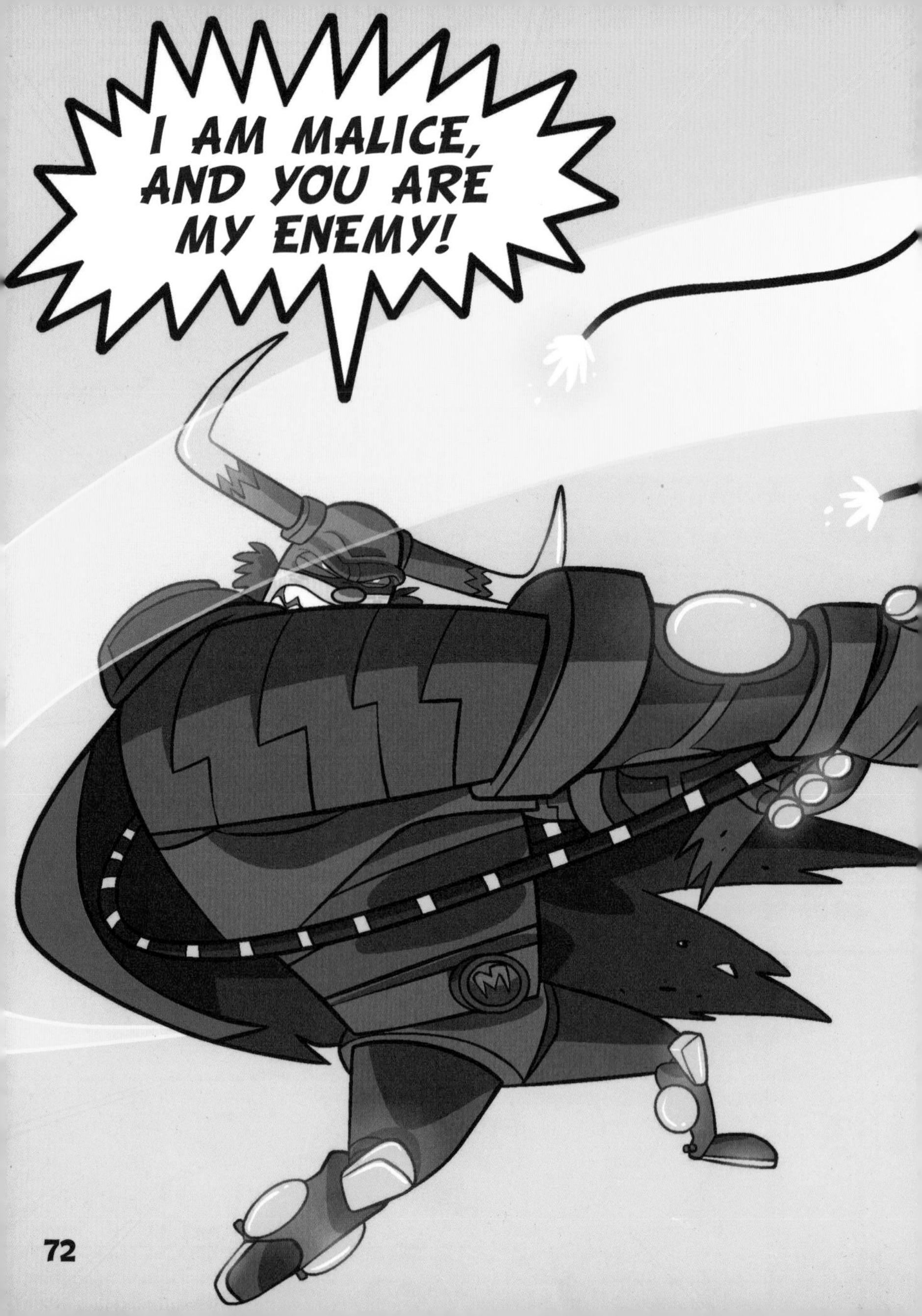
I AM MALICE, AND YOU ARE MY ENEMY!

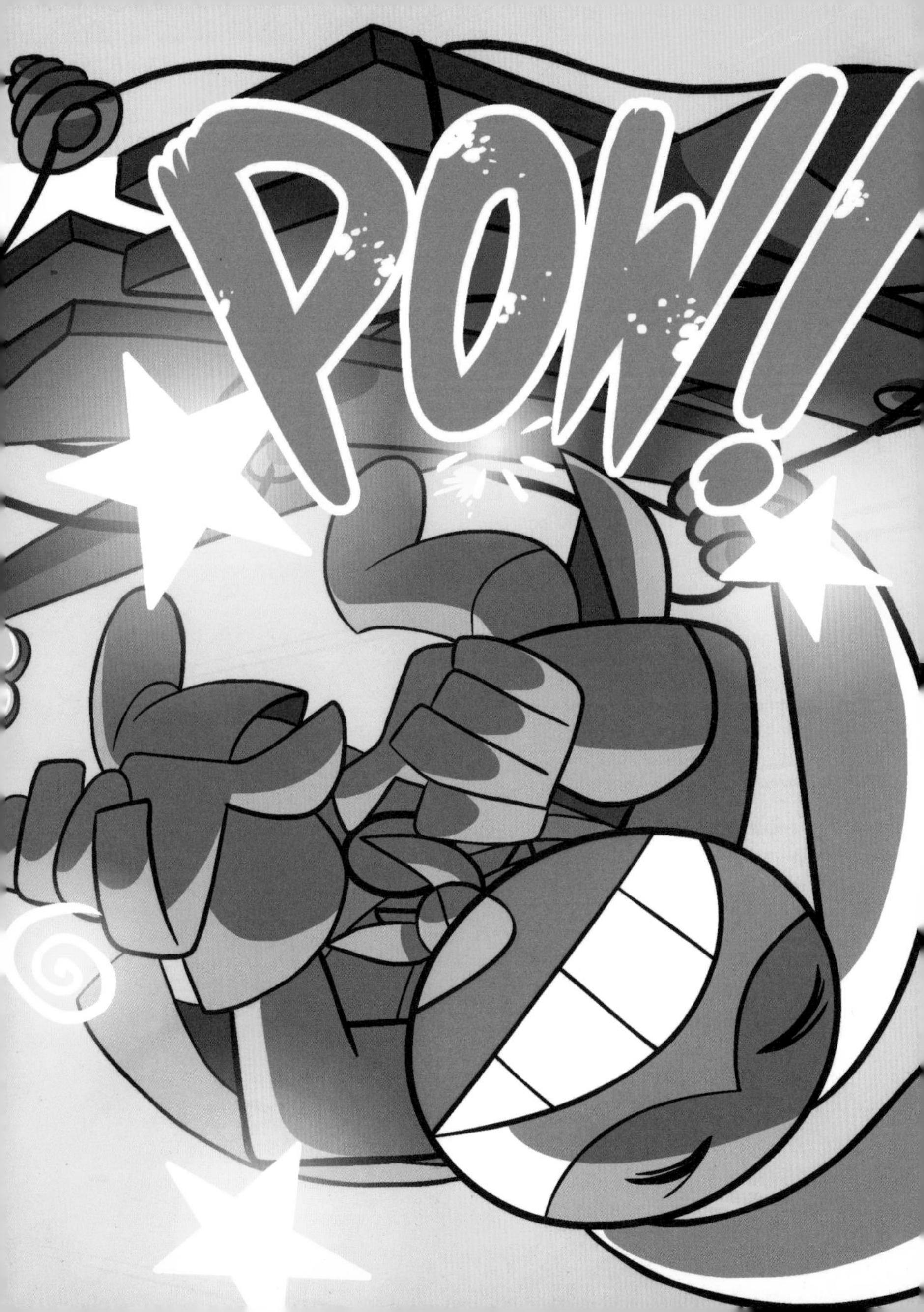
POW!

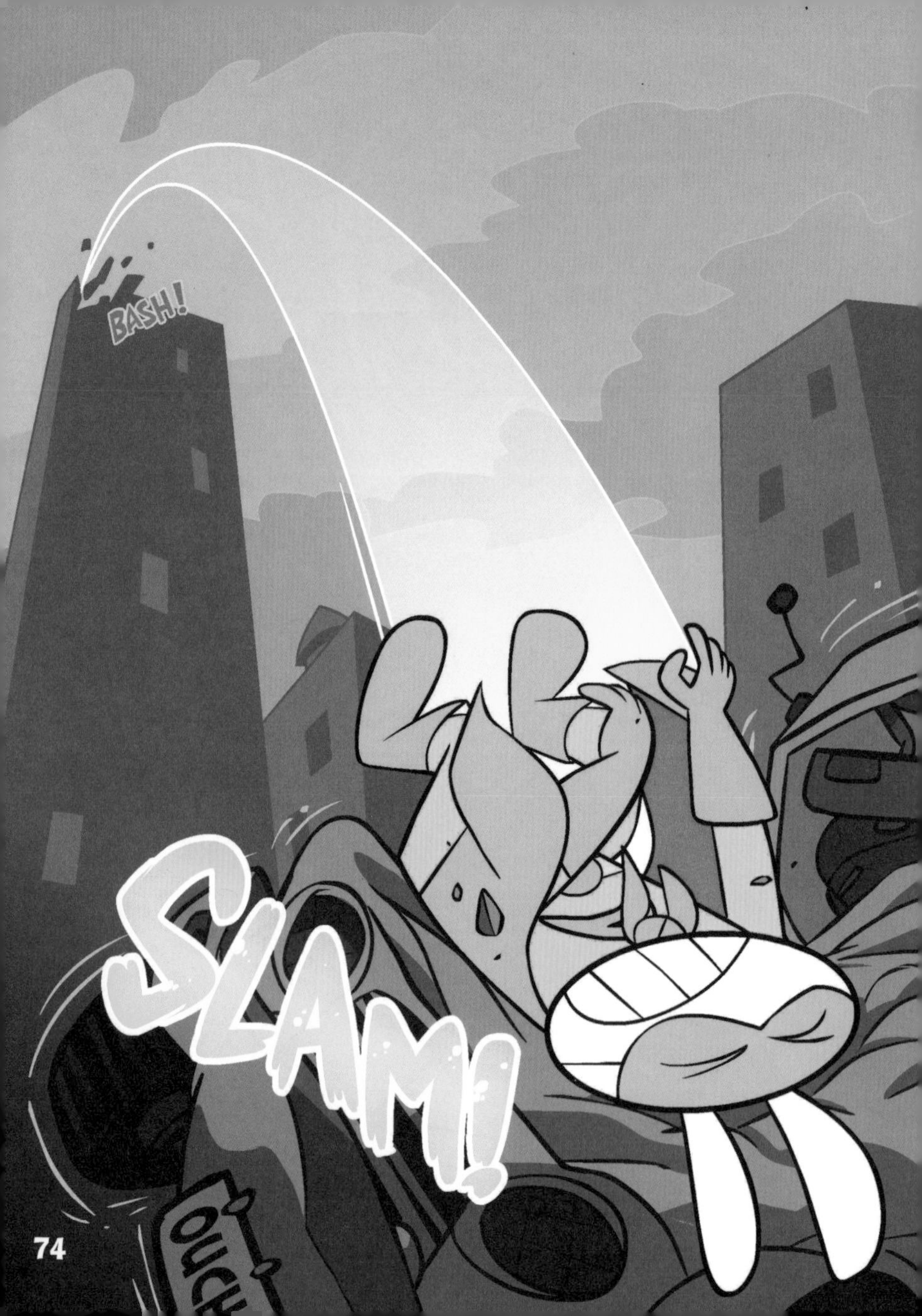
BASH!
SLAM!
OUCH

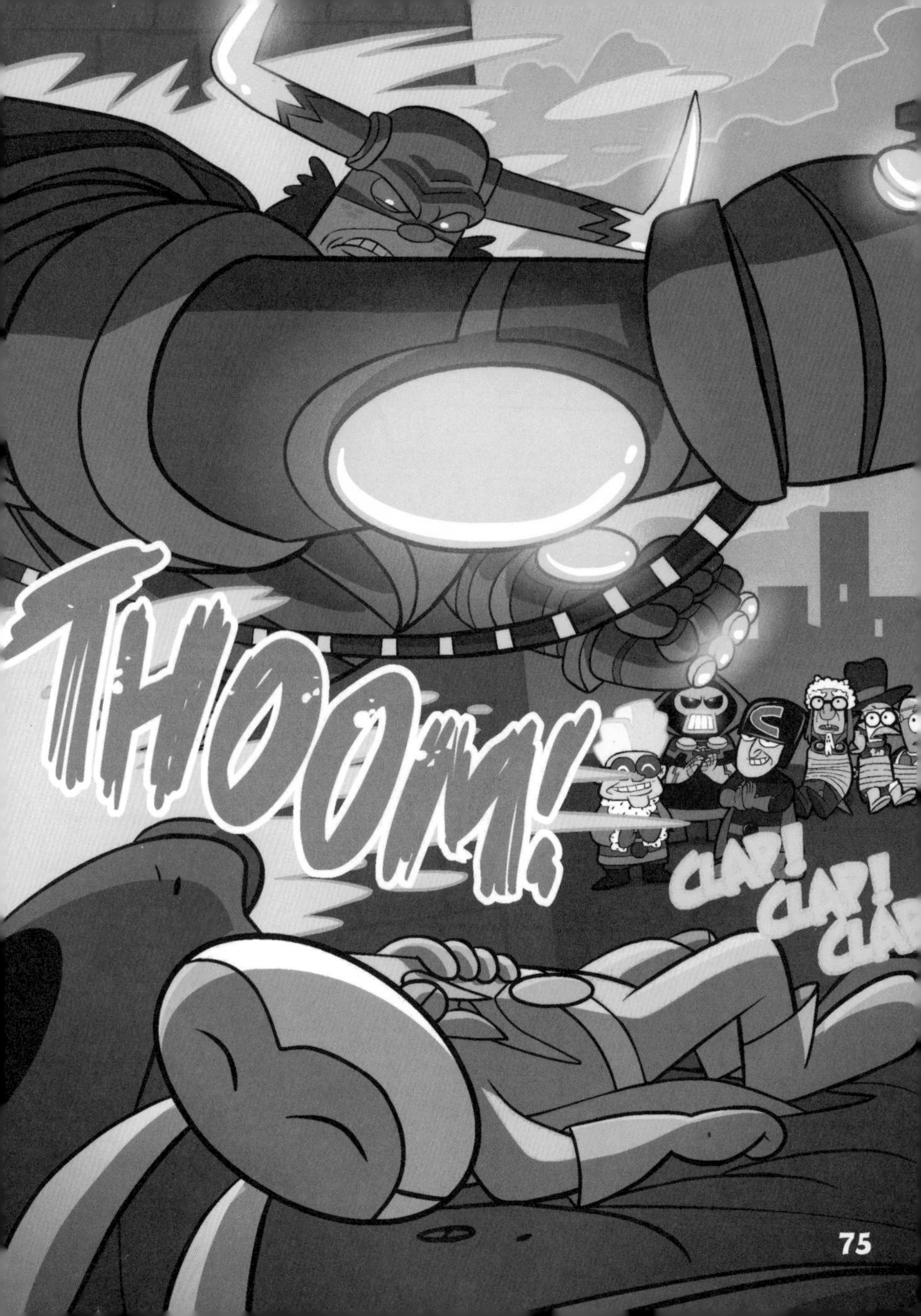
THOOM!
CLAP! CLAP! CLAP

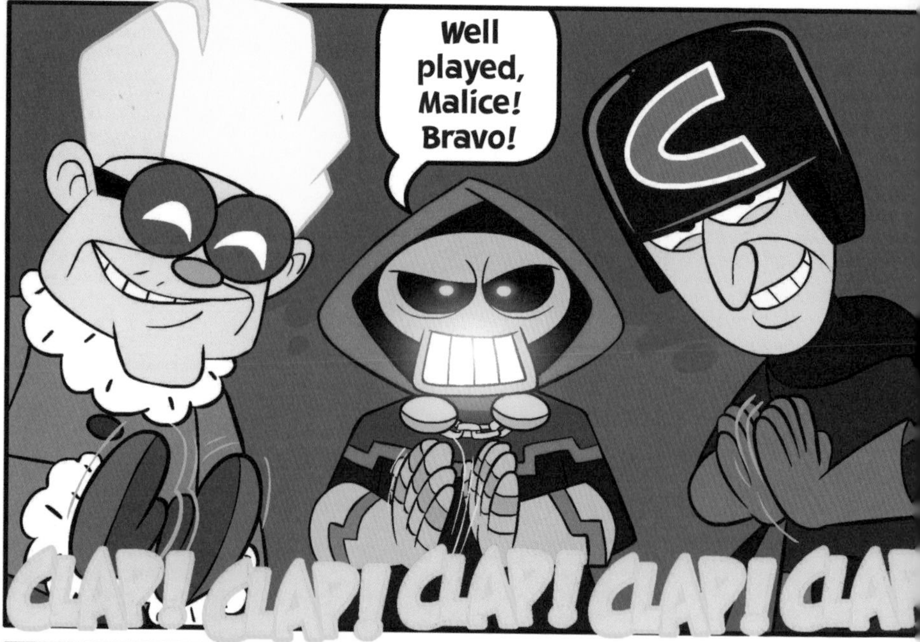
Well played, Malice! Bravo!
CLAP! CLAP! CLAP! CLAP! CLAP!

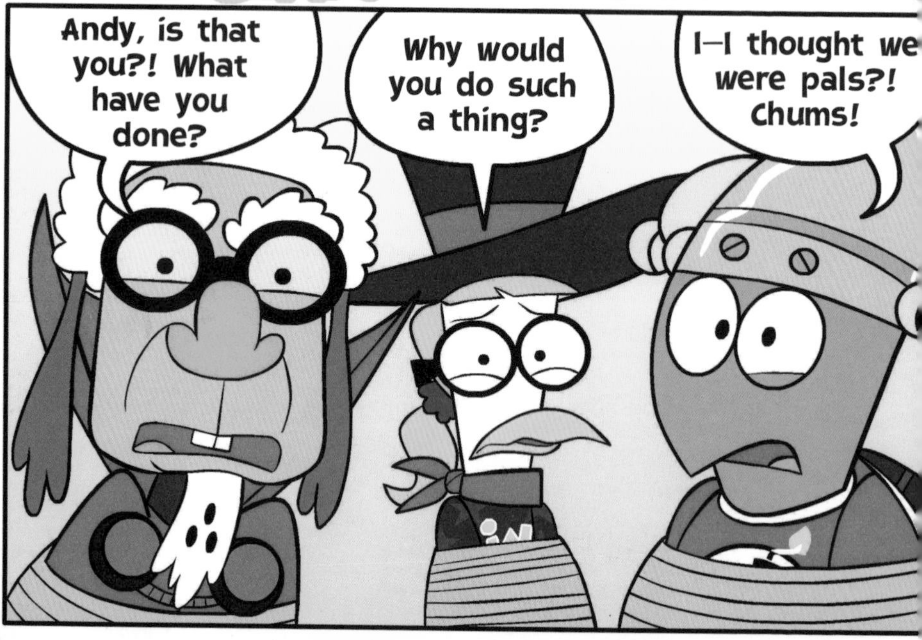
Andy, is that you?! What have you done?
Why would you do such a thing?
I—I thought we were pals?! Chums!

77

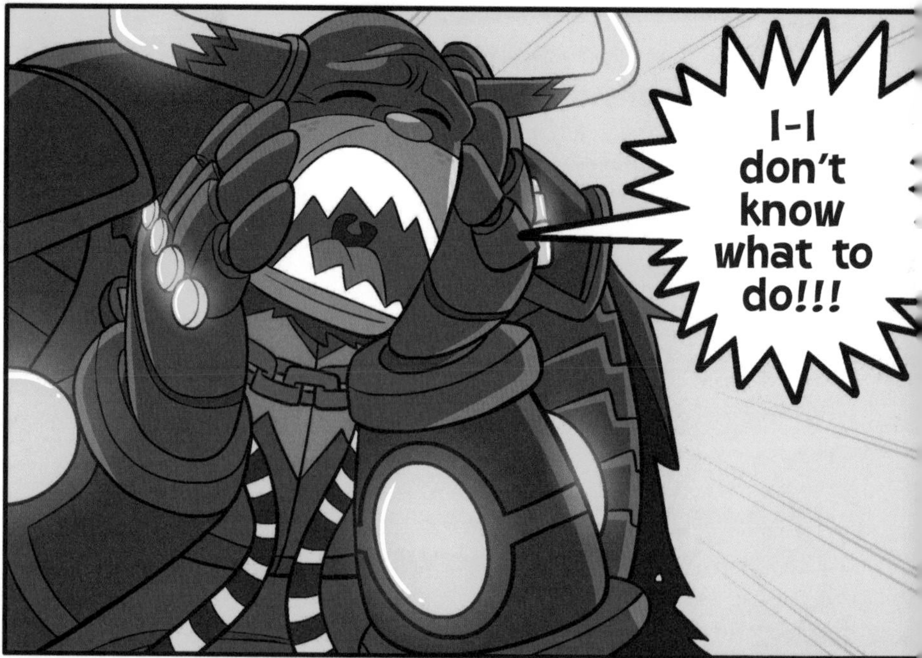
I-I don't know what to do!!!

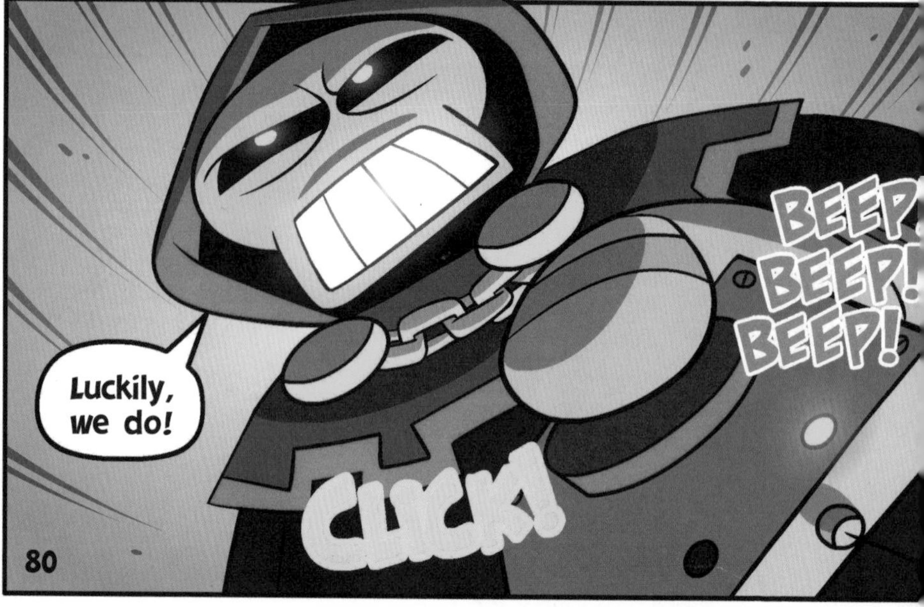
Luckily, we do!
CLICK!

81

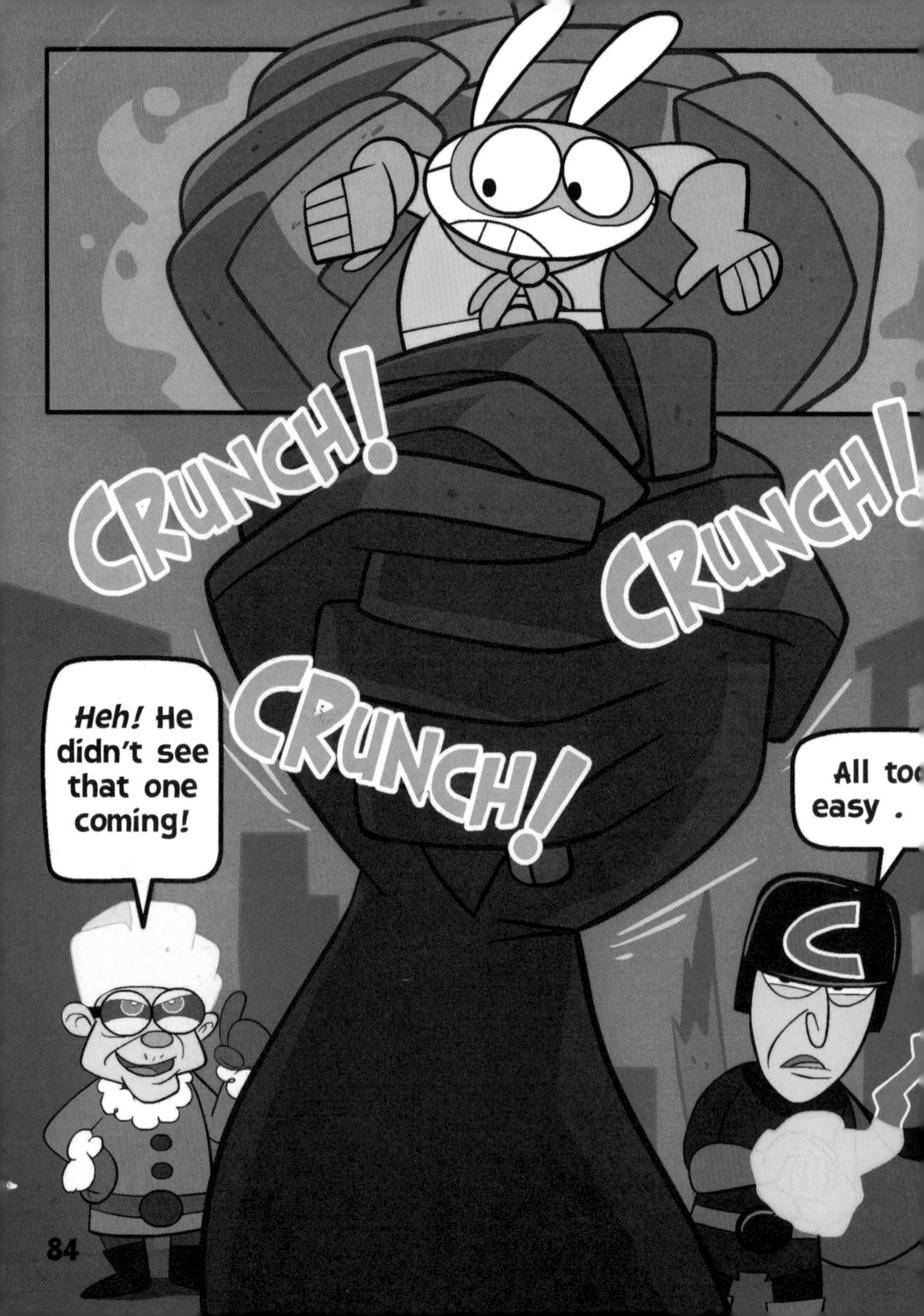
CRUNCH!
CRUNCH!
Heh! He didn't see that one coming!
CRUNCH!
All too easy . . .

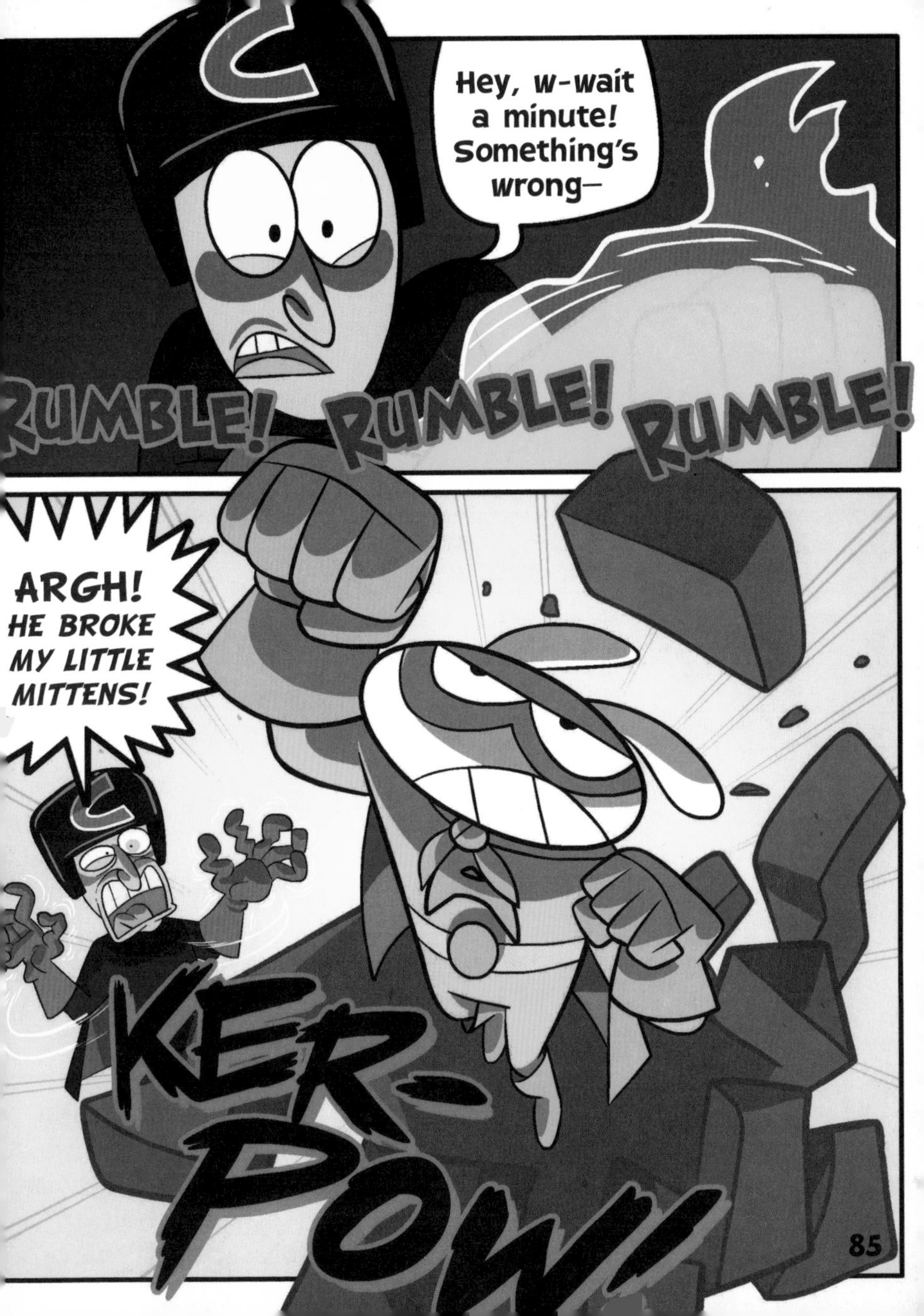
Hey, w-wait a minute! Something's wrong—
RUMBLE! RUMBLE! RUMBLE!
ARGH! HE BROKE MY LITTLE MITTENS!
KER-POW!

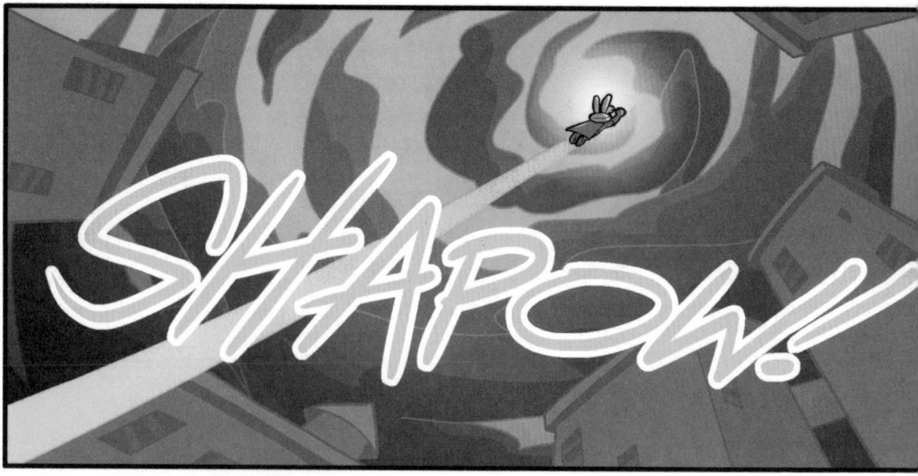
SHAPOW!

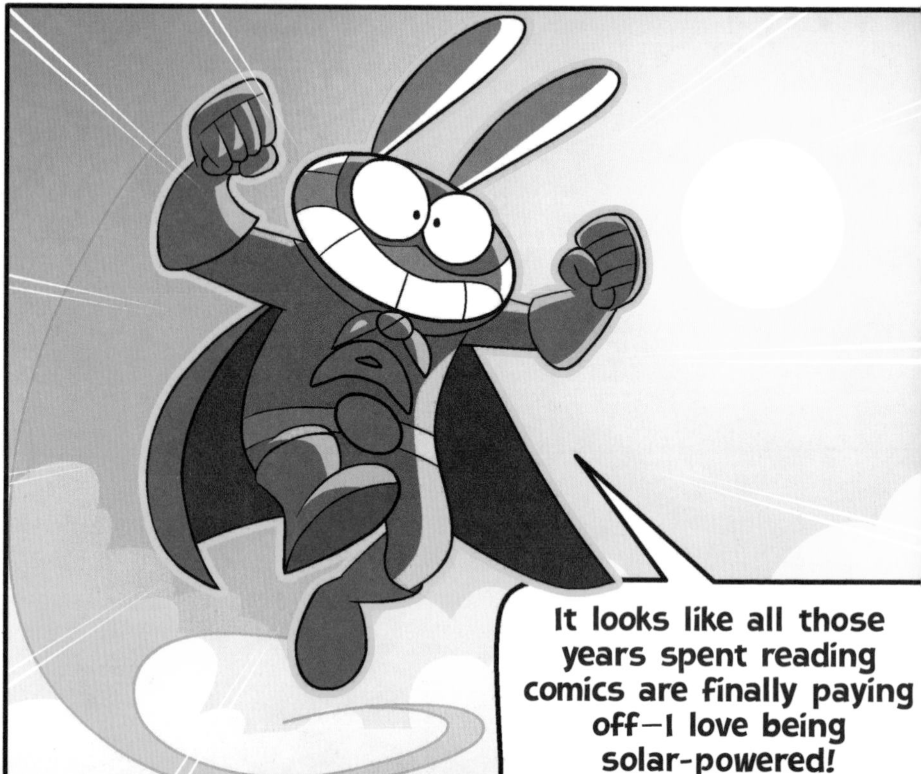
It looks like all those years spent reading comics are finally paying off—I love being solar-powered!

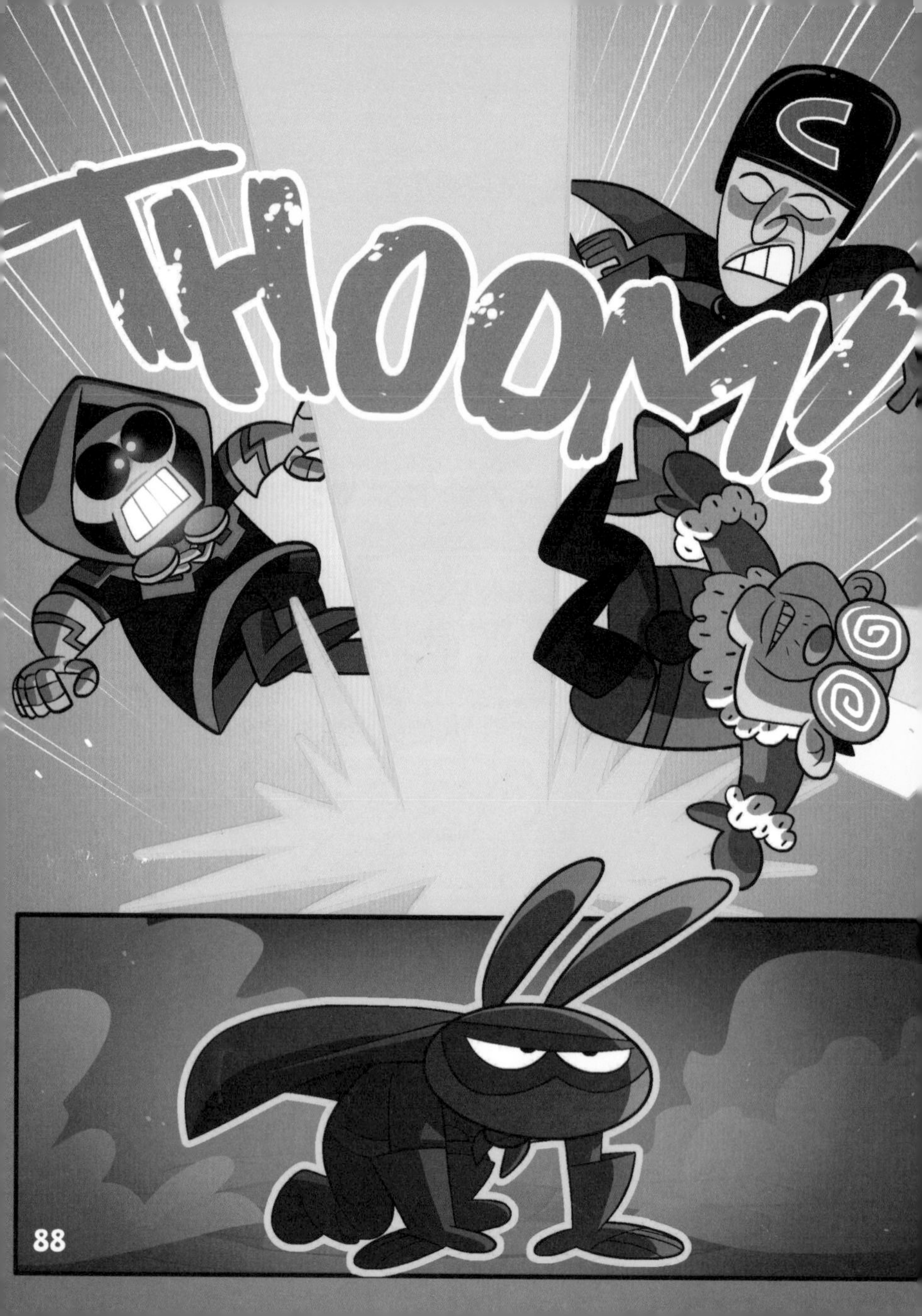
THOOM!

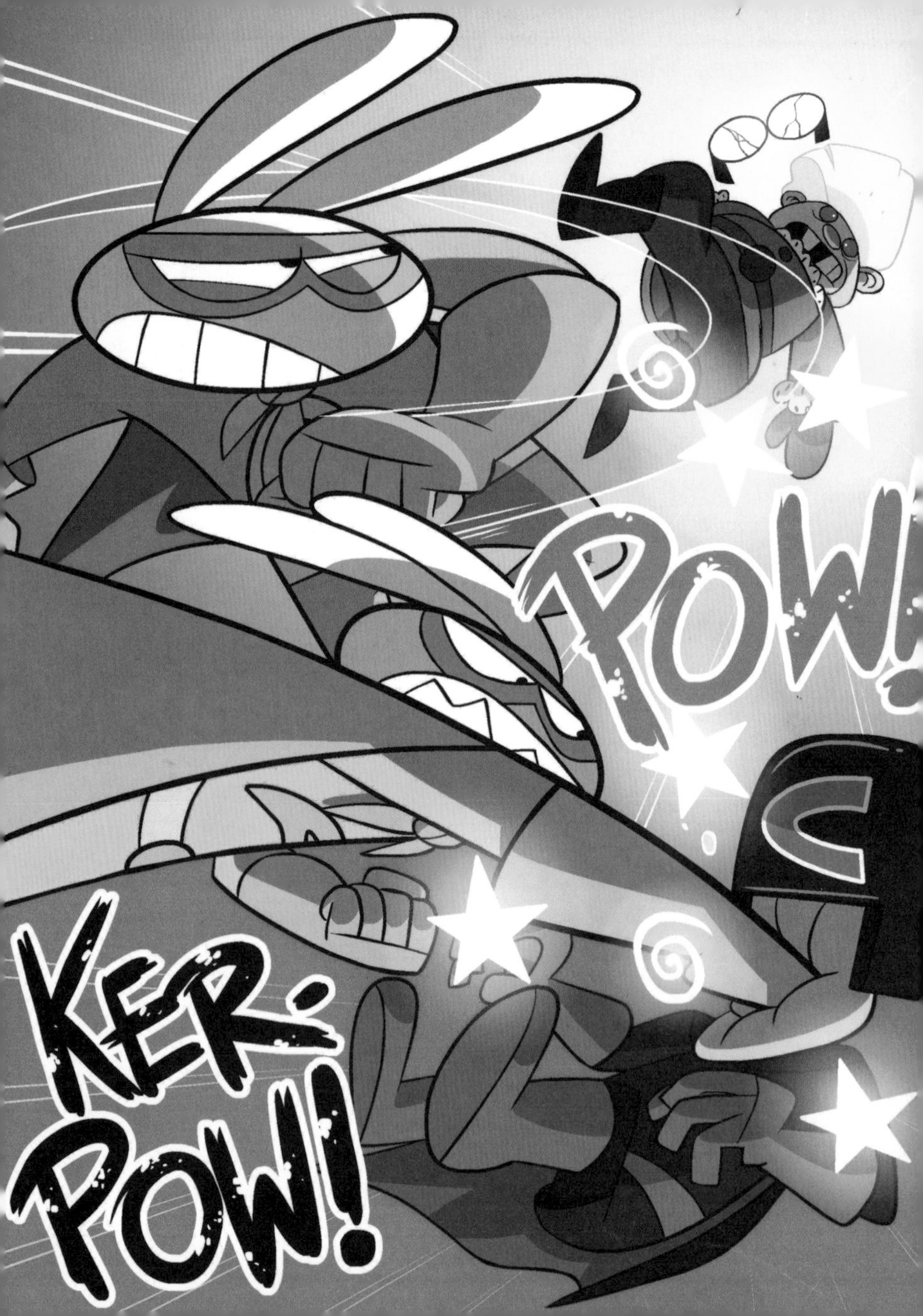
POW!
KER-POW!

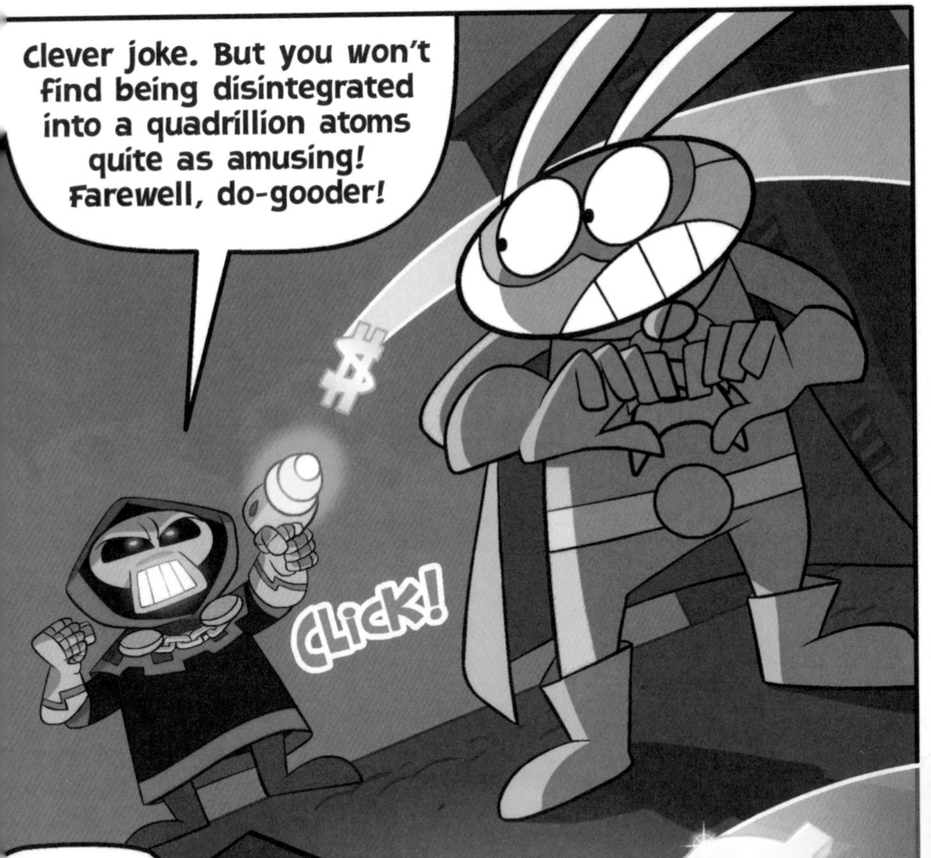
Clever joke. But you won't find being disintegrated into a quadrillion atoms quite as amusing! Farewell, do-gooder!
CLICK!
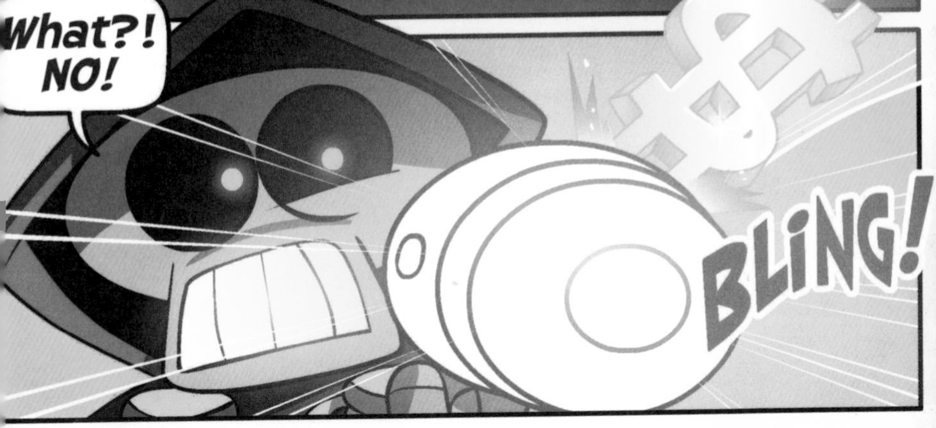
What?! NO!
BLING!